SO-AEW-118

Winner Books are produced by Victor Books and are designed to entertain and instruct young readers in Christian principles. Each book has been approved by specialists in Christian education and children's literature. These books uphold the teachings and principles of the Bible.

Other Winner Books you will enjoy:
Sarah and the Magic Twenty-Fifth, by Margaret Epp
Sarah and the Pelican, by Margaret Epp
Sarah and the Lost Friendship, by Margaret Epp
Sarah and the Mystery of the Hidden Boy, by Margaret Epp
The Hairy Brown Angel and Other Animal Tails,
    edited by Grace Fox Anderson
Danger on the Alaskan Trail (three stories)
Daddy, Come Home, by Irene Aiken
Patches, by Edith V. Buck
Battle at the Blue Line, by P.C. Fredricks
The Peanut Butter Hamster and Other Animal Tails,
    edited by Grace Fox Anderson
The Taming of Cheetah, by Lee Roddy
Ted and the Secret Club, by Bernard Palmer
The Mystery Man of Horseshoe Bend, by Linda Boorman

RALPH L. BARTHOLOMEW, father of two children, has taught grades four to eight in public school and Sunday School for 20 years. He attended King's College in Briarcliff Manor, N.Y. and received his BA and MA degrees from the University of Southern California. A photographer and free lance writer for many years, he has had over 50 short stories published. He has retired early from teaching to devote his time to writing about the things that interest him: missions in general—Wycliffe Bible Translators, Inc. specifically; winning others to Jesus Christ; adventure—exploring deserts; rock collecting; and gemology. Writing about the things he knows and loves gives his stories a touch of authenticity so essential to good stories.

"This book is dedicated to my mother who always believed I could do it."

Bart

GOPHER HOLE
TREASURE HUNT

Ralph L. Bartholomew

illustrated by Richard Mlodock

A WINNER BOOK

VICTOR BOOKS

a division of SP Publications, Inc.
WHEATON, ILLINOIS 60187

Offices also in Fullerton, California • Whitby, Ontario, Canada • Amersham-on-the-Hill, Bucks, England

Second printing, 1980

Scripture is from the King James Version unless indicated otherwise. Other quotations are from *The Living Bible* (LB), © Tyndale House, Wheaton, Ill.

Library of Congress Catalog Card Number: 77-80443
ISBN: 0-88207-479-2

VICTOR BOOKS
A division of SP Publications, Inc.
P.O. Box 1825 • Wheaton, Ill. 60187

CONTENTS

Chapter 1

A Brother for Jeff

Jeff Palmer gazed with satisfaction at the eight worm beds on the ground in front of him. Each bed was eight feet long, three feet wide, and one foot deep. Each was the home of at least 100,000 worms.

All Jeff's freckles moved toward his ears as he grinned. "I always did want a brother all my own," he said to his friend who stood nearby.

Terry Miller, Jeff's black buddy, frowned in amazement. "What does having a brother have to do with Mr. Tyler giving you his worms?"

Jeff laughed. "Right now I'm taking care of Uncle Marv's two beds, and for that he's teaching me how to grind gemstones. With a brother to help, I can easily take care of eight more."

"What makes you so sure that the missionary kid who's coming to live at your place will want to help?" Terry asked.

"Mr. Herron, his dad, showed slides at church the other night," Jeff answered. "In one, his son Mark was building a dugout canoe. Another slide showed Mark putting a new roof on a small building after a jungle storm. That guy really works."

Just then Mr. Tyler strode up. "Well, boys. They're going to bulldoze the worms away Saturday. So if you want them . . ."

"I want them, all right!" Jeff replied, his blue eyes shining. "You bet I want them!"

At that moment Jeff's 14-year-old neighbor, Ritter Colombo, appeared on his bike. Jeff's muscles stiffened as Ritter approached.

"I'll take 'em, Mr. Tyler," Ritter yelled, throwing up a cloud of dust as he skidded to a stop.

"Too late, Ritter," Mr. Tyler said. "Jeff here just said he wants them."

Ritter's face darkened like a stormy sky. "You've got two beds already," he told Jeff. "Why do you want eight more?"

"Th-those are Uncle Marv's," Jeff stammered. "I need my own to earn money. I've got to buy some Rainbow Ridge jasper."

Ritter frowned. "Jasper? What's that?"

"A rock from the desert," Jeff explained. "Uncle Marv's going to teach me how to grind and polish it into cabs. You know, stones for jewelry. I can sell them to the guy at the rock shop."

Ritter scowled. "What does a 12-year-old kid like you need money for, anyhow?"

"I'm saving up for a motorbike to use when Uncle Marv takes Terry and me to the desert."

"You don't need all eight worm beds," Ritter said, squinting at Jeff. "How about four?"

Jeff chewed his lower lip nervously. Ritter was older, a few inches taller, and a lot heavier than he or Terry. He looked huge as he sat there on his bike.

"Well, Ritter," Mr. Tyler broke in. "I guess it's a case of first come, first served. If you'd been here first, would you have given Jeff four of the beds?"

Ritter muttered angrily as he spun his wheel around and started off. All Jeff could hear was, "Get even," but that was enough. Of all the few billion people in the world, why did it have to be Ritter who wanted his worms?

"Thanks, Mr. Tyler," Jeff murmured. At least the problem was solved for the moment. He and Terry picked up their bikes to leave. "My Uncle Marv will help me get the worm beds home."

Although the Southern California sun was plenty hot, and the air smoggy, Jeff and Terry raced their bikes down the dirt road to Aunt Matilda's—Aunt Matty, everyone called her. Jeff had lived at her tiny farm since he had come from Ohio, two years before when his parents died.

As the boys rode along, they talked about the days ahead. "Will we ever have *fun!*" shouted Jeff. "Mark and you and I can go swimming in the town pool. We can visit the Opal Club with Uncle Marv. We can . . ."

"Go hiking in the mountains together," Terry added, his short legs pumping the bike like mad.

"Yeah. And remember, you promised you'd take me to explore those old gold mines too. Having a third guy along will be even better. Just in case . . ."

Terry frowned. "I don't know about that gold mine stuff."

"Hey, maybe Uncle Marv will take us all rock hunting in the desert. How about that?"

"Great!" Terry answered. Then, after a pause, he

asked, "Say, where did you say Mark came from?"

Jeff got real quiet. "Colombia, in South America," he murmured. "That's where I belong. That's where I should be right now."

Terry almost fell off his bike. "You should be where?"

"In Colombia. Right now," Jeff answered.

Terry's face was all frowns as he tried to figure that one out. Just then the boys came to the dusty driveway that led into the farm.

Not that it was used as a farm anymore, but there was still the big old barn out in back of the house Jeff shared with his aunt. In the barn was an apartment where the handyman and his wife used to live, and behind the barn was an overgrown orange grove where hundreds of gophers lived. The boys sped around to the back of the small house.

"They're here!" Jeff cheered as he spotted an old Ford parked between the house and barn.

Dropping their bikes, the two boys thundered into the house like a couple of elephants crashing through the African bush.

"Land sakes, boys!" Aunt Matty wheezed as they nearly knocked the tiny woman down. "Slow up a little, won't you?"

The visitors were just coming out of the living room. First came Mr. Herron, a big, sandy-haired man. Then came a small, dark-haired woman with friendly eyes, followed by a boy about the age of Jeff and Terry.

"I hear you talked your aunt into letting us use the apartment in the barn," the man said to Jeff as he held out his hand. "I guess helping us that way puts you on the missionary team, doesn't it?"

Jeff shook his hand. But he was looking at Mark, the boy who would be his "brother" all summer long.

"Let me introduce my family," said Mr. Herron. "Ruth, my wife, and our son, Mark."

Jeff grinned and said "Hi" to the boy.

But Mark stared right through Jeff, as if not seeing him at all.

"Shake hands with Jeff," Mr. Herron said, taking Mark's hand and holding it out.

Then it was Jeff's turn to stare. He felt cold inside, unable to move.

"Jeff!" Aunt Matty snapped. "Watch your manners."

"Oh . . . oh, yes. Hello."

Jeff held out his hand. Mark's fingers were cold, his hand limp. Jeff squeezed his hand slightly, then dropped it. "A-and this is Terry Miller," he said, looking over at his friend.

Slowly Jeff and Terry moved back, out of the room, out the door. Jeff felt as if he were lost in a thick, gray cloud. Both boys slumped down on the picnic bench in the yard.

"The Herron boy. He . . . he . . ." Jeff couldn't finish his sentence.

"I know," Terry murmured uneasily. "I guess we won't be playing much with him this summer."

"Or raising worms, either," Jeff said bitterly.

"His eyes. It's like they don't see you at all," said Terry thoughtfully. "Kind of like the kids in the special class at school—the TMR kids."

"What does that mean, anyhow?" asked Jeff.

"Trainable Mentally Retarded, I think," Terry answered.

"But . . . but I don't get it!" Jeff said. "I always thought God took special care of missionaries. How come they have a TMR kid? Couldn't they just pray, and . . ."

Terry shrugged. "I don't know. Maybe being a missionary isn't as easy as we thought."

Just then Aunt Matty led the Herron family outside. They talked a bit. Then Mr. Herron came over to where the boys were sitting.

"Mr. Herron," began Jeff. "Mark . . . ?"

"He had an accident," replied the missionary as he sat down. "Remember I said in church that we were praying for a special kind of place to stay?"

"What did you mean?" Jeff asked.

"Mark's doctor says that the best therapy for Mark would be to live with someone his own age. Someone to play with. Someone to work with. Someone who'd be like a brother to him."

Jeff turned his face so Mr. Herron couldn't see how he felt.

"Jeff, your aunt says you want a brother," the man went on slowly. "Mark . . ."

Jeff looked towards the distant mountains. "No . . . no . . . no . . . no!" he whispered. "Not Mark!"

Just then Mrs. Herron called. "Jim, Mark's lost his clay marbles again."

"Clay marbles?" Terry asked.

"They were given to us for Mark by an Australian trader in the jungle," Mr. Herron explained. "But when

Mark saw them he wouldn't let us keep them. He insists on keeping them himself in a leather pouch tied around his wrist."

Quickly Mr. Herron got up and headed for the house. The boys followed.

"But what are they?" Jeff asked.

"We don't know," Mr. Herron told them. "The trader said he'd write and tell us. But he did say that whatever happened, not to let Mark lose them."

Quickly, the three looked through every room. They found nothing. "I think I know where they might be," Terry said, suddenly dashing back into Aunt Matty's living room.

He came back into the kitchen, grinning. "I found them under a sofa cushion," he said. Jeff took the lumps from him and looked at them. They were heavy, yellow, and almost round. Then he gave them to Mr. Herron.

"Thanks, fellows, for your help," Mr. Herron said.

"Why don't you just take them away from Mark?" Jeff wanted to know.

"When he discovers they're gone, he won't stop fussing until he finds them again," the man explained.

Back at the car a few minutes later, Aunt Matty helped make arrangements for them to move into the apartment in the barn. Jeff's uncle Marv, who lived at the edge of town, would help them with his pickup truck in the morning.

A few minutes later, Jeff and Terry were alone again at the picnic bench under the maple tree.

"A TMR kid for a brother?" Jeff muttered. "Brother, or bother?"

"I know what you mean," Terry said. "That's too bad."

But something else was puzzling Jeff. "Hey, what about those clay marbles? I wonder . . ."

"Yeah. What's so important about them?"

Chapter 2

Jungle Accident

For awhile, Jeff and Terry just sat, each thinking his own thoughts. Jeff found it hard to take in all that had happened in the last few minutes. Suddenly Terry got a puzzled look on his face.

"Jeff, what did you mean when you said *you* should be in Colombia right now?"

"My parents were going to be missionaries there, but they never got to go. It was all my fault too."

"Your fault? What do you mean?" questioned Terry.

"When my dad quit his job to finish Bible school we had to sell our boat," Jeff began, "then our trailer."

"You had to kind of cut back on things?" Terry asked.

"Not only cut back, I was going to have to swap going to a newly built school for the heat, the stinging insects, and those awful diseases out there in the jungle. 'Man,' I said, 'Forget it!' "

"You said that to your folks?" asked Terry.

"Not exactly," Jeff answered, "but they got the message. One day they borrowed a boat and took a lunch out to one of the islands. They were going to spend the day, praying together about going to Colombia."

Terry frowned. "And when they came back, you'd changed your mind?"

"They never came back," Jeff murmured. "They probably never noticed the storm coming up till it was too late. They must have been trying to beat it home. The police said they really must have been traveling when they hit."

"Hit? Hit what?" asked Terry.

"A log underwater," Jeff answered in a hushed voice.

"But didn't they have life jackets on?" asked Terry.

"Sure. But they were killed instantly."

For a moment Terry was silent. Then he said, "Jeff, no way was it your fault."

"They never would have been out there if I hadn't been so mean and stubborn." Jeff felt the tears flooding his eyes. "They thought I was a Christian, but I wasn't. Oh, I went to church with them every Sunday, but I'd never asked the Lord Jesus to be my Saviour, to forgive my sins."

"But you have since, haven't you?" asked Terry.

"Yes, at the funeral," Jeff said slowly, remembering back. "But it was too late then."

Terry frowned. "Hey, you can't go on living with that monkey on your back."

"Monkey?" Jeff asked with a puzzled look.

"That's an expression," Terry explained. "When you're carrying around an awful load of worry, some people say you've got a monkey on your back."

"Like that dream I have every night?" Jeff wondered.

"Nightmares too? That's bad." Then Terry thought a minute. "That's why you want to help the Herrons so much?"

"Yeah. Maybe back in Colombia they can do the work my parents should have done—you know, teach the people about Jesus and all."

"Yeah. But I still say you're wrong to blame yourself."

Jeff went on as if he'd never heard his friend's words. "Maybe I could give them my $20,000."

"Your *what?*" asked Terry, his eyes wide with surprise.

"$20,000. You know, my dad's insurance money. Aunt Matty says it's supposed to be for college or something like that."

Just then Ritter appeared. He seemed to materialize out of the bushes between his place and Jeff's. Around his neck was a strap holding field glasses.

"That guy that was just here. Is he going to be your new brother?" he sneered. "Duh . . h . . h!"

Jeff's temper flared. "He can't help being that way. He was in a bad accident."

"What are you doing, spying on us?" Terry demanded.

Ritter grinned. "Got to know what's going on, don't I?" Then he turned to Jeff. "Guess you won't be needing those worms now, will you?"

Jeff felt trapped. Suddenly he had an idea. "Hey, Terry. You live two houses down the road. How about you helping take care of the worms?"

Terry held up his hand. "Sorry, Jeff. Remember, I've got to work around our place. Four hours a day, Mom says. If I help you, that'll leave no time for swimming, going to the beach or anything else."

"See? Better give them all to me," Ritter gloated with a victorious smile.

"I can still take care of at least three," Jeff argued. "You can have five. No more."

Ritter's smile turned sour. "I say all of 'em."

Jeff bristled. "Five!"

Ritter turned to go. "You'd better phone Tyler. Tell him I'm coming over."

Jeff and Terry glared at Ritter's back as he moved away.

"Let's hope that's the last we see of him," Terry whispered.

Almost as if he'd heard, Ritter turned. "Oh, by the way, I'll be over to borrow your book on worms. I want to ask you a few questions too."

"Oh, no!" Jeff groaned. No way would this be the last of Ritter.

Suddenly Terry perked up. "Hey, Jeff. Let's head for the swimming pool. We can't just mope around here all afternoon."

"Sure. We'll pass Mr. Tyler's place on the way. We can stop and tell him then."

After a swim, supper, and a little TV, Jeff headed up to bed in his tiny second-floor room. But instead of lying awake daydreaming of the fun Mark, Terry, and he would have all summer, Jeff thought of the way things had turned out.

Yes. Jeff was one of God's children now, but sometimes he wondered about things. Oh, he'd never admit it to anyone, but he wondered why God had let his parents die. And now he was wondering why God had let Mark have an accident that left him retarded. Jeff couldn't figure it out.

He was still puzzling when he finally drifted off to

sleep. Then it came: the dream he'd had every night the past year since his parents had died. In the dream two people were speeding along in a boat. It smashed into something hidden below the waves. The people were thrown out. The boat would flip up, over, and fall down, down, down. Jeff would cry, "Mom! Dad! Watch out!" But the boat would crash as Jeff screamed out, "No! No! No!"

Jeff's own yelling woke him up. Sitting there in bed, he felt sweat pouring down his body. He blinked hard, trying to erase the picture he'd just seen. But it took time for the vivid scene to fade.

After a bit, he lay back. He tried hard to think of the next day. That was the day his new brother would come. Brother or bother?

Next morning before breakfast, Jeff put some seed into his homemade bird feeder which hung from the huge maple tree in the backyard.

After breakfast, Terry came over. Soon Uncle Marv drove his pickup truck down the long dirt drive.

Uncle Marv's big brown eyes looked kind and thoughtful as usual. His thick mop of salt-and-pepper-colored hair flopped down over his forehead almost covering his bushy eyebrows.

He didn't get out of the truck, though. His legs were small and twisted. He had been injured in a fire and, though he could drive, he had to have help getting in and out of the truck.

"You guys going to stand around counting billy goats on the mountain peaks?" he asked, "Or are you coming along with me?"

Jeff grinned. "We're coming."

Soon the three were headed south to pick up the Herrons' things. When they got there, the first person they saw was Mark. The small leather pouch was tied around his wrist, but the clay marbles were scattered on the ground. Mark was rolling them back and forth.

Suddenly Jeff felt as though he were being crushed deep inside. In a way he wished he could help Mark, but in another way, he didn't know how to act.

On the way back, Jeff asked if Mark had always been that way.

"No," said Mr. Herron, "It happened about six months ago. My wife and I had to make a trip down the river to another village. Mark begged to stay behind with his friend, the Australian trader. The man said he'd watch out for Mark, so we decided to let him stay.

"The next day Mark decided to climb a tree to get some fruit. He lost his footing and fell. He was unconscious, so the Australian radioed us and the doctor in another village. The doctor flew in a small plane to where we were, picked us up, then flew to our own village. Then we flew Mark to the mission hospital some miles away. After a long time, Mark regained consciousness." Mr. Herron stopped.

"That's what caused his . . ." Jeff didn't quite know what to say.

"His brain damage?" finished Mr. Herron. "Yes, but we're thankful the fall didn't cripple him in body too, or even worse, kill him."

"Will this end your missionary work?" Uncle Marv asked.

"We can't take Mark back to the jungle village. But

if there were a neurologist, or possibly some other specialist at the main mission hospital who could take charge of Mark's therapy, we could all go back. There are only two other choices: stay here or go back but leave Mark here."

Everyone was silent awhile as the old truck rattled along. Then Uncle Marv spoke. "Didn't you say at church that you had just a little more work to do before you would have the whole New Testament translated into the language of those jungle people?"

"Two or three more years, yes. That's all we need," said Mr. Herron with a sigh.

"It would be hard to leave Mark at a special home here while you went back, wouldn't it?" asked Terry.

Mr. Herron nodded sadly. "He needs us just now. We feel the Lord wants us to stay here with him, at least for a while. There's a chance the County Home for Retarded Children might take him. A private home would cost too much—about $24,000 for three years."

Jeff thought about the problem then said, "I can't understand. You were out there telling people about Jesus. Why didn't God take care of Mark?"

"Son, missionaries have their troubles too, you know. They get sick. They have accidents. Sometimes they even die on the field. They're people just like everyone else."

"But we thought," Terry began. "We figured . . ."

"I know," Mr. Herron answered. "You thought missionaries were sort of special favorites of God, that no harm ever came to them, that God always protected them, and that they had special privileges."

"Well, don't you?" asked Terry.

"We have one very special privilege," the missionary said, "and that is to take the Gospel to people who have never heard it before. Now, that's a real thrill, believe me, and a privilege. But otherwise we're ordinary people, just like you."

For a long time no one said anything. Then Jeff asked, "Mr. Herron, would you tell us about those round clay lumps Mark carries?"

"That's part of the same story. When the Australian trader learned Mark was so badly hurt, he nearly went crazy. Mark was like a son to him, and of course, he felt responsible for Mark's accident. Before we came home, the trader brought that pouch and tied it on Mark's wrist, telling him never to lose it."

"But what *are* those lumps, anyhow?" asked Jeff.

"He said he'd write us a letter about them, but we haven't received it yet."

Uncle Marv looked as if he were thinking hard as he asked, "Where in Australia did the trader come from?"

"Oh, some wild-sounding place in the desert of Australia. Hurricane Peak or Stormy Mountain. Something like that."

"Could it have been Lightning Ridge?" asked Uncle Marv.

"Lightning Ridge. That's it! The fellow did mining or something there."

"Hmmm," was all Uncle Marv replied as he speeded up.

Jeff knew that his uncle always speeded up when he was excited. *What does Uncle Marv know that's so exciting?* he wondered.

"I sure would like to take a look at those lumps some time," Uncle Marv said.

Soon they were back at Aunt Matty's. It didn't take long to unload the truck since the Herrons didn't have much.

When they were through, Mr. Herron went in to talk with Aunt Matty. Uncle Marv called the boys over to the truck where he was waiting.

"Whatever you do," he told them, "don't let Mark lose those clay lumps."

The boys promised, but they wondered why the clay lumps were so special.

"Oh, I nearly forgot," Jeff said suddenly, "Mr. Tyler's giving me three beds of worms. Could you help me move them in the truck, please?"

"Be glad to," answered Uncle Marv. "When do you want me?"

"Before Saturday morning?" Jeff asked.

"Let's see, I'm busy till Friday after lunch," said Uncle Marv. "Would Friday afternoon be all right?"

Jeff grinned. "Fine. I'll be ready!"

During the week, Jeff watched Mark a few mornings. That gave the Herrons some time to go grocery shopping. One day Jeff taught Mark how to fill the bird food cans high on the feeder. Another day he got out his old wagon and pulled Mark around the yard and out into the old, overgrown orange grove behind the barn.

When the smog began to blow in from Los Angeles, late in the week, Mark developed a cough. He began rubbing his eyes alot too, until they got all red.

Jeff felt hurt inside as he watched Mark. The boy

was like a small child. He didn't understand many things. But Jeff did his best to keep him entertained.

When Friday afternoon came, Jeff was ready. He had spent the morning rounding up shallow, wooden lug boxes from behind supermarkets. These boxes were good for carrying worms. Also by lunchtime Jeff had smoothed out a patch of ground behind the barn, and had built three frames, each three feet by eight feet by one foot deep. These frames would be the worm "beds."

All morning Jeff worked alone. The Herrons were away at a missionary conference. Terry was home doing his four hours of work, but he and Uncle Marv would come over right after lunch.

"Aunt Matty?" Jeff called as he plunged through the back door. "I'm ready to eat."

Quickly he headed for the kitchen sink to wash up. Suddenly he realized there was no food cooking. The table was not even set.

He turned the water off and listened. "Aunt Matty?"

No answer. Then he moved into the next room. Still no Aunt Matty.

The downstairs bedroom door was open. Jeff peeked in. Aunt Matty was on the bed.

At first he thought she was resting. Then he heard her gasping for breath.

"Aunt Matty!" he cried. "Are you all right?"

She tried to answer, but all she could do was struggle for air. Jeff felt like yelling for help. But who would hear?

"Shall I call Uncle Marv?" he asked.

She nodded her head "yes."

Jeff ran to the phone and dialed. "Uncle Marv, come quick. Aunt Matty can't breathe!"

"It's the smog," his uncle said. "I'll be right over."

Jeff went back, but he didn't know what to do to help.

"Phone hospital," Aunt Matty wheezed.

"For an ambulance?" asked Jeff.

His aunt shook her head "no."

"Are we going to take you there?" asked Jeff.

Aunt Matty nodded.

By the time Jeff had finished telling the emergency room they'd bring Aunt Matty right in, he heard the truck pull up by the back door.

"Jeff, you're going to have to get her out here by yourself," Uncle Marv told him. "You CAN do it. Now hurry."

Jeff raced back. Aunt Matty looked awfully white. He had to hurry. But how?

"I'll have to half drag you," he said as he sat her up.

Carefully he rested her head against his chest. Then he wrapped his arms around her waist. Backing up, he let her feet fall to the floor.

Jeff was surprised at how light Aunt Matty was as he dragged her to the door.

In another minute, he had her in the truck. Uncle Marv started off even before Jeff had shut the door.

"You'll have to hold her up. We'll head for emergency."

"I already called," Jeff puffed. "They said to drive up as close as you can. They'll bring out a stretcher and oxygen as soon as we get there."

Uncle Marv was driving about as fast as he could

through town, but when Jeff looked at Aunt Matty, he yelled, "Hurry! She can't breathe!"

When they got there, two men with a rolling stretcher were waiting. One pulled the door open and, reaching past Jeff, pushed an oxygen mask over Aunt Matty's face. Almost immediately she seemed to relax a bit and breathe better.

Jeff slipped out, and the men lifted her onto the stretcher. "I'll park and be back to sign her in," Uncle Marv told them.

"It's Matty Jensen, isn't it?" one of the young men asked. "She's been here before. It's the smog."

Jeff waited in the truck. About a half hour went by before his uncle returned. "I'll take you home. Then I'm coming back to be with her."

Slowly, Uncle Marv started, then shifted into reverse. "She's getting old, Jeff. A couple more attacks like this, and her doctor will make her go to a rest home."

"But what'll happen to me?" asked Jeff in fear.

"Don't worry. We'll figure something out."

"But you've got such a tiny place," Jeff said. "And your daughter and her three kids are with you."

"Well . . ." Uncle Marv wrinkled up his forehead till his big bushy eyebrows came together.

As they pulled into the drive again, they saw Terry waiting. "We'll take the lug boxes over to Tylers'," Jeff said. "We'll have them full when you come."

"I don't know when I'll get back. I've seen Matty have a lot of attacks, but this is the worst one yet."

As Uncle Marv left, Jeff filled Terry in on what had happened. Then the two boys tied the empty lug boxes to wagons behind their bikes and headed for Tylers'.

When they got there, they saw that Ritter had already taken his five beds. Only three were left.

Since most of the worms would be near the surface, the boys skimmed off the top few inches of each bed. Afterwards, they piled the heavy, wooden boxes near the fence.

After a quick supper at Terry's, they came back to wait. Still no Uncle Marv. Finally at dark, they left. The three beds were still in Mr. Tyler's yard.

Jeff was alone that night. Not that he minded. The only thing that bothered him was Ritter. If Ritter knew he was alone, he might try something.

Jeff didn't always remember to pray, but that night he did. Bowing his head before tumbling into bed, he murmured, "Dear Lord, please help Aunt Matty to breathe OK again. Please heal her asthma. And, Lord, please may Ritter not bother me. For Jesus' sake, Amen."

The next day Terry came over early. Jeff had already made toast and eaten his cereal, so they phoned Uncle Marv.

"Yes, Aunt Matty is much better," said Uncle Marv. "She'll be home sometime today. I'll meet you at Tylers' later," Uncle Marv promised.

Right away the boys headed over to Tylers'. But even before they arrived, they could hear the powerful motors of the huge earth-moving machines. Tylers' farm was being leveled! They were putting in a tract of homes!

Ritter was there too, watching. "You lied!" he yelled at Jeff.

A tractor roared in front of them. "You just didn't want me to have those beds."

The three worm beds crumpled before their eyes. "All those worms down the drain!" Ritter yelled.

The huge machine smashed through everything, leaving nothing but bare ground where the worm beds had been.

"Just because of you!" Ritter fumed.

Jeff wished he could evaporate like the steam from a coffee pot. "Uncle Marv had to take Aunt Matty to the hospital," Jeff explained. "He never got back in time to help."

The way Ritter glared, Jeff knew he didn't believe him. He wondered what would have happened if Uncle Marv hadn't pulled in just then.

"Sorry I couldn't get here last night, fellows," he said. "But I'll make it up to you somehow."

"We saved 20 boxes full," Jeff told him. "They're over by the fence."

"OK. Load 'em up."

After they had finished, the boys climbed in. Uncle Marv frowned. "Say, weren't you figuring on selling those worms to buy Rainbow Ridge jasper?"

"Yes," answered Jeff sadly.

"Hmmm," Uncle Marv mused. "How'd you like me to take you out to the claim? You could dig your own jasper."

"Oh, would you?" shouted Jeff.

Terry grinned. "That would be super!"

Chapter 3

Storm in the Desert

The rest of Saturday was plenty busy. Jeff emptied the boxes of worms into one of the beds he had prepared. Aunt Matty came home from the hospital. She could take care of herself, but Mrs. Herron did look in on her every now and then.

Sunday after church and dinner, Jeff and Terry tore over to Uncle Marv's on their bikes. He phoned his friend who owned the Rainbow Ridge jasper claim up in the desert.

"Sure," the man said, "take all you want!"

The rest of the afternoon the boys spent rounding up rock hammers, coal chisels, work gloves, rock bags, and other odds and ends.

When they were almost finished, Uncle Marv looked over at Jeff and chuckled. "What do you think you're going to do? Bring back the whole mountain?"

Jeff frowned. "What do you mean?"

"Well, look at all those boxes you're bringing. You could put a ton of rocks in all those."

Terry laughed. "He'd make a good scout. Always prepared."

Early Monday morning they got started. First they

took the freeway east, then north. Once through the mountain pass, they took a narrow, winding road deep into the high, upper desert.

Light tan sand covered the hills and plains on both sides of the road. Light green sage grew here and there. A sprinkling of Joshua trees (looking like stubby, 15-foot, fat-limbed monsters) dotted the landscape.

"This is what I wanted a brother for," Jeff said, as he watched the passing scenery, "to do things like this with."

Terry laughed. "You always got me, old buddy."

Jeff reached over and punched his arm. "Sure, but . . . "

"I know what you mean," said Terry. "I'd like one too—a guy who'd be with me 24 hours a day."

Jeff was silent. Then he said, "I took care of Mark while the Herrons went to the store the other day. I showed him how to fill the cans on the bird feeder with seed."

"Could he reach up without spilling seeds all over?" Terry asked.

"He tried," Jeff said. "He really tried."

After about three hours of driving, Jeff started to get the wiggles. "Aren't we ever going to get there?"

Uncle Marv laughed. "I thought you'd never ask. Fact is, that's Inyokern in the valley ahead. China Lake is over on the right. Just over those mountains is Death Valley. Does that tell you anything?"

"Just that we're in mighty hot desert country, right in the middle of summer," Jeff panted.

"Yeah, but this is high desert. Shouldn't it be cooler?

And didn't you say it showers up here in the afternoons sometimes?" asked Terry.

"Right," Uncle Marv answered. "Look toward the west."

Already clouds were forming over the mountains. Jeff knew they'd have to head toward them to get to the claim.

Just then Uncle Marv slowed down, turned off onto a dirt road to the left, and coasted to a stop.

"Boys, I used to come up here with the rock club. There were always plenty of fellows around if I needed help. Today there's only you two and me, and I can't do much with these crippled-up legs of mine. Now, there's nothing to worry about if we take it slow and careful. I told the owner I'd phone him when we got back out to the main road. If I don't call by five, he'll come looking for us. Just the same, I think we'd better ask God's protection. Jeff, would you like to start?"

Before he closed his eyes, Jeff glanced around. He could tell that the dirt road ahead didn't get much traffic. They'd be going in beyond those hills in the distance. Then there were the clouds. In the desert, they could spell big trouble. But Uncle Marv knew what he was doing. He'd been here many times before. And they were going to pray, weren't they?

"Dear Lord," Jeff began, "Thank You that we can come out here to hunt jasper. Please help us find some good rocks so I can polish them up and sell them. And please don't let us have any flat tires or engine trouble or anything like that. In Jesus' name, Amen." Terry prayed next. Then Uncle Marv.

When they were through, Uncle Marv explained, "Most people get in trouble speeding over these bumpy roads. But us? We're going to take it real easy."

"Say, Uncle Marv, didn't you go to school and study all about rocks and things?" Terry asked.

"I studied gemology, my boy. All about gemstones," the man replied.

"He's setting up a lab in his garage," Jeff told Terry. "He's going to make man-made black opal."

"Black opal? What's that?" asked Terry.

Uncle Marv grinned. "Oh, that's one of the most expensive gemstones in the world."

They rode on in silence again. The bumpy road through the hills and down into the "washes" never seemed to end. The places called washes were dry now, of course, but could fill up fast when it rained.

They had to go about 20 feet down to the bottom of one wash, then across. It was pretty wide too—about as wide as a football field. Then they went up the slope on the other side. Jeff shuddered. He'd hate to be caught down there in a storm.

Finally up ahead they saw a hill. It was steeper than the rest. The road seemed to stop at its base.

"Here we are!" Uncle Marv chuckled. "I've spent many a happy day looking over this hill."

"But where's the claim?" Jeff wanted to know. "Where are all the holes?"

"Halfway up the hill is a flat place. Diggings are up there."

The boys started to tumble out even before Uncle Marv stopped. "Hold it, fellows. I'll be puttering around here. There's jasper on the surface all around. You fellows take it easy. Remember, I can't come get you if you get hurt."

"We won't try anything dumb," Terry promised.

By the time the boys had scrambled up the slope, they were puffing hard and their legs ached.

"Oh, man, I've got to take a break." Jeff slumped to the ground.

Terry collapsed beside him. "Hey, what does this jasper stuff look like, anyhow?"

"Oh, some is clear, but most of it is yellow or orange or red or black. The colors sort of come in streaks in this stuff here."

For a few minutes the boys just puffed and looked. From where they sat, they could see miles in every direction. Barren, treeless valleys were at their feet. Mountains were in the distance, all around. Overhead, the sky was clear and blue. But to the west, over the mountains, clouds were beginning to thicken.

"I wish I'd known Mark before his accident, "Jeff said thoughtfully. "I'll bet he'd have been great." Then he frowned. "I really wonder. Why did it ever have to happen, anyway?"

Terry shrugged. "There's always Romans 8:28. 'All things work together for good to them that love God.'"

"'All things,'" Jeff echoed. "I guess you REALLY have to have a lot of faith to believe that."

"Yeah. 'All things.' Like your folks too," Terry said.

Again they looked over the scene below. "You know, taking care of Mark once in a while is OK with me. But trying to be a brother to him—. I just don't know."

"They said it would help him get better quicker, remember?" Terry said.

Jeff only nodded.

Just then Terry picked up a rock. Idly he tapped it with his rock hammer. "Hey, look here! All brown and orange. Shiny too."

Jeff studied the piece. "That's jasper, all right. But the colors aren't right. You need a better pattern, one that would look good in a ring or in some other jewelry."

By then the boys had their strength back, so they headed over to one of the many holes in the side of the hill. For the next two hours they used their picks, crowbars, and sledge hammers, prying rock out of the ground.

"Hey, Jeff," Terry called from where he was digging a few feet away. "Know something? We're the very first human beings ever to see these rocks. Man, isn't that something?"

"That's one thing about rock hunting. You never know what you might find," Jeff called back.

Just about the time Jeff thought he was getting into a pocket of really good rock, the boys heard the truck horn. Looking down, they saw Uncle Marv waving at them.

"Lunchtime, I guess," Terry said. "Shall we leave our stuff here?"

"Better take it all with us. Just in case," said Jeff.

Back at the truck, Uncle Marv had sandwiches and pop ready. While they ate, he studied the rocks the boys had found. "You can make good cabs out of that," he told Jeff.

"What are cabs?" Terry wanted to know.

"Cabochons," Uncle Marv explained. "Curved, oval

shapes used in jewelry. You've seen stones set in rings, bracelets, and all. They're cabs."

It didn't take them long to wolf down the food, gather up their stuff, and start to go again.

Uncle Marv studied the sky. "Boys, I hate to say this, but I don't like the looks of things."

The boys gazed at the puffy white clouds over the mountains nearby. They were dark on the bottom and getting darker all the time.

"I didn't know it rained in the desert in the summer," Terry said.

"The worst storms are usually in summer. Come on, boys. We'd better hurry and pack up."

Again Jeff fearfully glanced at the sky. He had heard of cloudbursts—when so much rain fell that washes became instant rivers.

A few minutes later Uncle Marv had stowed his crutches in the back, the boys had loaded up their tools and rocks, and they were off.

Wistfully, Jeff stuck his head out the window and looked back. "So much good jasper left."

"And so close too," Terry moaned.

A few minutes later Jeff noticed a flash of light in the sky. "Hey, was that lightning?" he said.

Uncle Marv slowed down to look. "See that grayness hiding the top of that peak? Rain. Heavy rain."

"But it's plenty far away, isn't it?" Terry wondered.

"The water runs off this way," Uncle Marv said.

"But the sand's dry. Doesn't the rain just soak right in?"

Uncle Marv frowned. "If there's a cloudburst, the ground can't absorb it fast enough."

"Is that when there's a flash flood?" Jeff asked uneasily.

"Mmmmm," answered Uncle Marv. "Sometimes the water comes down fast, just as if a dam broke upstream. It all comes down at once. We'll have to hurry."

Uncle Marv wasn't kidding. Jeff clung to the door. Terry jammed his feet against the floor. But still they got thrown around the cab like Ping-Pong balls in a tournament.

Jeff glanced over. He'd never seen Uncle Marv drive this way before. His hands grasped the steering wheel so hard his knuckles were white. His whole body hunched forward as he glared out at the road ahead. He reminded Jeff of a motorcycle racer he had seen once on TV.

Suddenly they came to the big wash. Twenty feet deep, at least. Uncle Marv paused. Glancing west again, he grimaced. "It's coming closer. We've got to hurry."

Carefully, he eased the little pickup down the sloping side. Then he headed across. With the wind whipping up the dry sand, it was hard to see the edges of the road.

Suddenly Uncle Marv jammed the truck into low gear and revved up the motor. Jeff noticed the stretch of loose sand ahead.

At first the truck lunged forward. The motor roared. The tires spun. Then, slowly, slowly, they came to a stop.

Quickly Uncle Marv jammed it into reverse. "This fine sand . . ."

Jeff couldn't hear the rest over the roar of the motor. The truck moved a foot or so. Then Uncle Marv threw it into low. But nothing happened.

"Hey, what's that smell?" Terry wondered, sniffing.

"That's the clutch. It's getting a real workout," said Uncle Marv.

Finally the man turned off the key. "Boys, we've got to get out of here fast. Put down the tailgate and pile rocks in the back, and hurry."

Instantly the boys tumbled out and scrambled around the back.

"Hey, Uncle Marv, there's hardly any rocks here," Jeff yelled.

Grabbing his crutches, the man got out and hobbled around. "You'll have to weigh down the back. Fill those boxes with sand. Both of you lift them on. Make it quick."

As they started working, Terry asked, "Think we'd better run for it?"

Uncle Marv squinted at the road ahead. "Take me a good 10 minutes to walk out, and I'm too heavy for you to carry." Then he studied the clouds, heavy with rain. The storm was moving their way fast.

He crutched his way back to the cab, got in, and started the motor. By now the boys had about six full boxes in the truck. "Throw in the shovels, then climb on the back," shouted Uncle Marv.

The boys climbed on and the truck inched forward. The weight of the boys and the sand on the back was helping.

"Hey, Terry. You hear that roar?" Jeff yelled.

"Must be thunder," his friend answered.

"But thunder stops. That sounds like a freight train coming our way," said Jeff.

Slowly but surely they moved ahead. As soon as they were on solid ground, Jeff felt Uncle Marv speed up.

"Terry! Look!" What Jeff saw made him freeze with fear.

Roaring down the wash was a wall of water three feet high. Nothing, but nothing, was slowing it down.

Jeff glanced over his shoulder. Would they make it out of the wash in time?

The water tumbled toward them, smashing everything in its way.

"Oh, Lord," Jeff prayed, aloud, "please get us out of here! Fast!"

The water was almost to them when he felt the front of the truck hit the slope.

Jeff bounced. His hand slipped off the side of the truck. He felt his body floating in air. He grabbed again for the side, but only his wrist smashed against it.

"Lord, help!" he yelled.

His hands hit the side. Desperately he grabbed hold, and just then it felt as if a huge hand covered his, clamping his fingers tight.

The wall of water thundered by, reaching out for him as it passed. It tackled his legs, almost sucking him off the truck. But he managed to hang on.

In another second, they were up and out of the wash, and just in time. As the water swept past, it carried with it rocks and bushes—everything in its path.

Slowly the truck coasted to a stop. For a moment the boys just sat, unable to move.

"I'm glad he didn't come," Jeff murmured.

"Mark, you mean? Me too," said Terry.

Slowly the boys slid off the tailgate and headed toward the cab. Uncle Marv was slumped over the steering wheel, exhausted. At last he heaved a sigh and lifted his head.

Jeff could see his face was soaked with sweat.

"Thank God, we made it!" was all Uncle Marv said.

Chapter 4

News from Headquarters

It was about 5 o'clock when they reached Uncle Marv's place. There Jeff unloaded the chunks of jasper he had found. After that Uncle Marv drove Terry home first, then Jeff.

Quickly, Jeff unloaded his tools on the picnic table near the back door. After Uncle Marv left, he turned to put things away.

Just then Mrs. Herron came out of the apartment, her dark eyes troubled. "Jeff, did something happen this afternoon? I mean, did you have an accident or something?"

Jeff stared. "How did you know?"

"Mark was sleeping right after lunch. That's the only quiet time I have for my devotions," she explained. "Suddenly I felt the Lord telling me to pray for you. You were in great danger."

"A flash flood," Jeff said. "We nearly didn't make it. But, I don't understand. How?"

"Sometimes mothers get that feeling about their children," she explained gently. "Maybe God let me be your mother for just a little while this afternoon. I prayed hard, Jeff. You were in real danger. Then, suddenly it was over; I was sure that you were safe."

Jeff slumped down on the picnic bench. "I was holding onto the side of the truck," he said, half to himself. "We hit a bump. I flew up in the air and nearly fell off. I tried to grab, but my hands were upside down. I smashed my wrist against the side. Then suddenly my fingers grabbed. It seemed like a larger hand clamped over mine. I couldn't have let go if I wanted to."

"The hand of God!" Mrs. Herron whispered, smiling. She patted Jeff on the shoulder.

In bed that night, Jeff thought a lot about what had happened that day.

The next day after breakfast he knocked at the Herrons' door. As he waited, he heard a few sparrows high in the trees, chirping for their breakfast. When Mrs. Herron came to the door, he asked, "Can Mark help me fill the bird feeder?"

Mark came out grinning. "Br . . . br . . . "

"Birds," Jeff told him. "Feed . . . the . . . birds."

"Burrrr . . . "

"Birds. Birds. You'll get it yet. You're getting better every day. Keep trying," encouraged Jeff.

Mark grinned. "Burrrr . . . "

Later that morning, Jeff took Mark with him to his worm beds. First he spread a thin layer of horse manure over the worm beds. After that he watered them carefully.

"Worms can't eat anything dry," he told Mark.

"And they have to live where it's damp. If their bodies dry out, they'll die."

Mark listened. Jeff felt he was trying to understand.

Trying. That was good. Even if he didn't get it all, he was trying.

After taking care of the worms, the two boys went behind the barn. The orange trees, like ragged soldiers all in a row, looked mangy from lack of care. Right now, Jeff thought, it looked more like a gopher playground. Mounds of soft dirt were everywhere. Mark liked to dig in the loose dirt that led down to the gophers' underground burrows.

As Jeff watched, he caught himself thinking about the strange happenings of the day before. Mrs. Herron had prayed just for him—like a mother.

Sure would be nice having a mother again. Aunt Matty was too old, but Mrs. Herron?

After a while Jeff took Mark back for lunch. Just then Terry came pedaling up the drive on his bike.

"Hey, Jeff, the mailman left two letters for the Herrons at our place by mistake. Airmail letters from Colombia."

"Bet they're pretty important," Jeff said as they headed over to deliver them to the Herrons who were out in the yard just then.

Mr. Herron opened one and began reading it. "This is from the head of our jungle base," he announced. "He wants me to teach a language course in mid-September."

Mrs. Herron beamed. "Oh, Jim. That's wonderful."

"Do you teach other missionaries how to translate?" Jeff asked.

"He's learned a lot about tonal problems in our languages," Mrs. Herron explained. "In our villages, if you say a certain word in a high tone, it means 'corn.'

But if you say the same word in a low tone, it means 'snake.' "

"It's very easy to say, 'Would you have a little snake with your monkey meat?' " Mr. Herron added, laughing.

"Sounds like kind of a hard language to learn," Terry said.

"It wasn't easy, I can tell you," Mrs. Herron replied.

When Mr. Herron finished the letter and looked up, Jeff asked, "Think you can make it?"

The big man sat down on the picnic bench. "The doctor says Mark is improving, especially since he's been here with you. But he won't be ready to go back by September."

"But couldn't you leave him here while you go down to finish your translation work?" Jeff wondered.

Mr. Herron frowned. "We're not leaving him. Besides, if he couldn't get into the County Home, it would cost about $24,000 for a place for him here in the States for three years, and we just don't have that kind of money."

Mrs. Herron moved close to her husband. Gently she put her hand on his shoulder. "I don't want to leave our dear son any more than you do. But God has given us a job to do, Dear. Did you ever think that it just might be God's will that we leave Mark here while we go back and finish?"

"Mark needs us," Mr. Herron snapped. "We stay with Mark!"

Jeff looked surprised at Mr. Herron's tone. Usually he spoke softly to his wife. But this time he sounded harsh. Like a flash, Jeff remembered how his dad had sometimes raised his voice like that about something he thought he should do. His mother used to kid him gently.

"Who are you trying to convince, Honey?" she would say. "Me or you?"

Mrs. Herron went on, her voice soft. "If Mark had died, we would be back on the job right now. Should we do less because God spared his life?"

Mr. Herron squirmed uncomfortably, but he didn't answer.

For a while Jeff thought hard. Maybe Mrs. Herron was right. Maybe God really did want them to go back without Mark. But that meant they would need $24,000, and they'd need it fast. That was a lot of money. But maybe there was a way. After all, weren't they taking his parents' place down there? Weren't they teaching the jungle people about Jesus, God's Son, the only One who could forgive their sins? Now Jeff knew what he must do. Somehow, some way, he must help the Herrons round up that cash.

The other letter was from the Australian trader. Jeff felt his heart pounding as he waited for the news.

"Here it is," the missionary said. "The trader says, ' The yellow clay lumps were found deep in a mine in the black opal fields of Lightning Ridge, Australia. They just might contain valuable black opal. I hope they do, for then they can help pay for some of Mark's medical expenses.' "

"Black opal?" Terry burst out. "Hey, Jeff, isn't that the kind of gem Uncle Marv's trying to make in his lab?"

"Yep! And is it expensive!" said Jeff excitedly.

Mr. Herron went on reading. " 'Take them to a reliable gem cutter. Tell him to grind slowly, very slowly. Use plenty of water. Never let them get warm.' "

"Maybe that's the way the Lord will supply the money for Mark," Jeff said.

Mr. Herron frowned. "Slow down, Jeff. In the first place, we're not leaving Mark anywhere. And in the second place, there probably isn't anything in those lumps of clay anyway. And in the third place, I once heard a preacher say, 'Don't expect a miracle if there's a means available.' "

"A means?" the boys asked.

"A means—a way to do something yourself. For example, if you break your arm, don't just pray that God will perform a miracle and heal you instantly, right then and there. Go to a doctor. He's a 'means' you can use."

"Don't you believe in miracles?" Jeff asked.

"We believe in them, all right. The Lord used a miracle to help you and Terry and Uncle Marv in the desert yesterday. And we've certainly prayed for a miracle for Mark. But I think God uses them sparingly, just once in a while. Right now we're trying to use every means God might supply."

"What means?" Terry asked.

"For one thing, we take him to a neurologist once a week. That's one means. And you and Jeff are another means."

"Us, a means?" Jeff was puzzled.

"Your help. Your care. It's doing Mark a world of good. Just the therapy he needs."

"Well," Jeff thought, "just the same, I think those

clay lumps could be a means too, if there's opal in them."

Terry joined in. "Yeah, what other means is there?"

"None in sight, right now," Mr. Herron said. "But if the need should arise, the Lord will supply." Then he called, "Mark, come here, please, Son."

From where he was sitting in his wagon, the tall blond boy got up and moved toward his father. The brown leather pouch was hanging as usual from his wrist.

"May I look at your marbles, please?" his father asked.

He peered in. Suddenly he flipped the pouch upside down on the picnic table. Marbles rolled everywhere. Jeff and Terry slapped their hands on the table to keep them from rolling off.

"Hey, those are the glassies I gave him," Terry said. "But where are the lumps of clay?"

Gently the man turned to his son. "Sit down, Mark. Can you remember? Where are the lumps of clay? Where did you put them?"

Jeff and Terry stared. It was sad to see the boy trying so hard to think.

"Where—are—the clay—marbles?" Mr. Herron asked slowly.

Mark just frowned. His mind was blank. He just couldn't remember. Jeff wondered if he could even understand his father's questions. And even if he could, it was plain that he couldn't remember.

"We'll find them," Jeff promised, brushing his red hair out of his eyes. "They've got to be around here somewhere."

That afternoon the boys helped the missionaries turn the apartment inside out. They searched every possible corner. But no clay marbles.

"How about the old bathtub out behind the barn?" Jeff wondered. "Mark always likes to splash around there."

"And the pile of hay," Terry added. "He was there too. And the worm beds."

"And the gopher holes he dug up the other day," added Jeff.

It was 5 o'clock before the boys had finished their hunt. They began with nothing and ended with nothing—nothing but a lot of places where they knew the clay marbles were not to be found.

That evening Mr. Herron phoned Uncle Marv and told him all about the letter. Uncle Marv said that when they found the clay marbles, he'd be glad to grind and polish them. He hoped they'd find something good in them.

The next morning began like many others. Jeff was up early and dressed. He made his bed, then turned to dash downstairs.

But he happened to notice a small booklet on the table by the bed lamp. It was a book from the Bible, the book of Proverbs, but it was written in modern-day language.

Jeff stopped short. It didn't make sense to rush down to try to do something for Jesus and never bother to read His Word. And certainly trying to help the Herrons get back to Colombia was doing something for the Lord.

Jeff reached for the booklet, then settled back to

read. This was his second time reading it through. Now he was up to chapter three.

When he came to the sixth verse of chapter three, he knew that was his verse for the day. Carefully he copied it on a small card. He'd stick it in his pocket and try to remember to pull it out now and then. That way he might be able to memorize it. "In everything you do, put God first, and He will direct you and crown your efforts with success" (Proverbs 3:6, LB).

After a short prayer, Jeff hurried outdoors to the apartment to get Mark. Together they filled the cans with birdseed. Then Jeff asked, "Where did you put the clay marbles? Can you remember?"

Mark frowned, trying hard to think. Then he turned and looked back at the cans on the feeder.

"No. Not the birdseed. I mean the marbles. You had them in the leather pouch around your wrist." Jeff spoke slowly and plainly. "The marbles. Did you put the marbles somewhere?"

Again Mark looked toward the cans he had just filled. Jeff turned away, wondering why God would ever let such an accident happen. He guessed there were things he'd never understand.

Right after breakfast Terry skidded his bike to a halt in the dirt by Jeff's back door.

"Let's go out behind the barn," Jeff suggested. "I've got something to show you."

When they got there, Jeff pulled out his card. "I'm going to memorize this verse today: 'In everything you do, put God first, and He will direct you and crown your efforts with success' (Proverbs 3:6, LB). Pretty good, huh?"

"Sure is," Terry murmured. "We're trying to help the missionaries, aren't we?"

"Yeah. And that sure is putting God first, so He promises to direct us."

Terry grinned. "And to crown our efforts with success!"

"Right. But one thing I'm learning. Working for God isn't always easy. We looked plenty hard yesterday, and we still didn't find those clay marbles."

For a minute they both just sat wondering. Then Jeff spoke. "Our teacher last year put up a poster. On it was written, 'When all else fails, stop and think.' "

Terry frowned. "You know, a Christian might say, 'When all else fails, stop and pray.' "

"Ha! That's funny," said Jeff.

"I don't see anything funny about praying," Terry said with a frown.

Jeff grinned. "No. I mean, isn't that what we usually do? Try everything else first? THEN we remember to pray."

"I see what you mean. Hey man, what do you say we pray first this morning?" Terry suggested. So the boys did. Terry prayed first. "Dear Lord, Thanks for the beautiful day. Thanks for giving us good minds and strong bodies. Thanks for giving us people to take care of us. Now, Lord, You know we'd sure like to find those clay marbles. Please help us figure out where to look. And may the opals in them be good enough to pay for a home for Mark while the Herrons go back to Colombia. In Jesus' name, Amen."

After Jeff prayed, the two boys walked slowly back to the house.

"Why don't we make a list of each place Mark goes?" Jeff asked. "Then when he has to rest after lunch, we can search all the places he's been. Maybe we'll find the clay marbles that way."

Jeff got a clipboard, a pencil, and some paper. Every place Mark played, Jeff wrote down on his list. After lunch he and Terry went out to the picnic table to think things over.

"Know where I think they are?" Terry said at last. "Buried in one of those gopher holes."

Jeff frowned. "Maybe you're right. Let's go see."

About an hour later they came back and slumped down at the table.

"You boys look kind of warm," Mr. Herron said as he came out of the apartment.

"We've dug up 21 gopher holes and sifted all the loose dirt," Jeff told him. "You know how many marbles we found? Zero!"

"Say, maybe you two better take a break. We're going down to the beach for the afternoon and supper. How about coming along?"

"Hey, that's swell," Terry said.

"We'll be ready," Jeff added.

The afternoon at the beach was fun—racing down the beach, splashing in the surf, lying in the sun and listening to the seagulls scream overhead.

But still, enjoy it as he might, Jeff's mind was churning with other thoughts, like all those gopher holes. There must be hundreds, maybe *thousands* of them. If the clay marbles were there, they would need help digging them up. If only Ritter weren't so mean, they could ask him to help.

As Jeff and Terry talked it over, Jeff shouted, "I've got it! What about the Tom Sawyer plan? You know, Tom was the guy in a book who had to whitewash a fence. He got all his friends to help. Remember?"

The rest of their time they spent planning. When they got home, Jeff phoned Mrs. Keller. She was the president of the Women's Missionary Society at church.

"Well, since you're doing it for the missionaries," she said, "I'll see what I can do. Phone me Saturday."

Saturday night Jeff did phone.

"I talked to your Aunt Matty," Mrs. Keller told him. "Everything's OK for Monday morning. Three of us women will be over at about nine."

"Oh, thanks a lot!" said Jeff. "I just *know* we'll find the clay marbles now."

Chapter 5

Treasure Hunt

By Sunday evening Jeff and Terry had made all the necessary arrangements. They had told the kids in their Sunday School class all about their plans, and some had promised to come. They also got the Garcia twins from school to help.

Mrs. Keller and two of her friends from the Women's Missionary Society at church were coming over with lemonade and lunch for the boys and girls. Aunt Matty wanted to help too, but she was sick again. So she said she'd do her part by praying.

When Monday dawned clear and sunny, Jeff just *knew* this was going to be it: the day of the great treasure hunt; the day they'd find the lumps of clay— lumps filled with fabulous black opal! Uncle Marv would grind and polish them. Then they would sell the opal for lots of money—money enough for a home for Mark while the Herrons went back to Colombia to finish their translation work.

By 9 o'clock a dozen kids had gathered at Aunt Matty's little farm. Soon they trooped out behind the barn into the orange grove. Jeff and Terry led the way.

"Oh, man! Look at all those gopher holes!" Kevin

exclaimed. "You mean we've got to dig up all of those?"

"The gophers dug 'em," Lisa quipped. "Why can't we?"

"Gopher *holes*?" someone asked. "Maybe we should call them gopher mounds instead."

Jeff headed toward the fence on the north side of the property. "Kevin, why don't you and Bill start here," he suggested. "Dig up every hole between the fence and this first row of trees."

Bill flipped his trowel up and caught it by the handle. "Exactly what are we doing, anyhow?"

"We want to dig out just the soft dirt," Jeff explained. "Then sift it through this half-inch screening we've got here. We're looking for six lumps of yellow clay. They're about the size of large marbles."

"You say there's opal in them?" Carol asked.

"Black opal, maybe," Jeff corrected.

"What opal?" Bill asked.

"Opal's a shiny gemstone found mostly in Australia and Brazil," Jeff said. "Most opal is white. The stuff that's black with patches of red, blue, gold, and all, is called black opal."

"It's rare!" Terry added, "and expensive too."

Bill laughed. "Then this really is a treasure hunt, huh?"

"Right. We're kind of treasure-hunting for God."

"Well, if you guys get out of our way," Bill kidded, "we can start."

Jeff and Terry went on to show the others the rows where they should dig. But even before they were done, Bill yelled. "Hey, you guys, I think we found 'em!"

There was a wild scramble as they all tore back to crowd around Bill and Kevin.

"OK, give me some room, will you?" Jeff yelled as he tried to push through the knot of kids.

Jeff studied the lumps carefully.

"Are they what we're looking for?" asked Lisa.

"Are they the right ones?" Bill asked.

Holding one of the lumps in the palm of his hand, Jeff tapped it lightly with Bill's trowel and it crumbled into dust.

"Aw, nothing but regular old dirt," Kevin grumbled.

Then Jeff took another. When he tapped, loose dirt fell off. Only a pebble was left. "I guess not, but keep trying."

Slowly the others moved back to their own diggings. Terry grinned as he left. "Can't win that easily."

By the time they had gotten the last two kids started, Kevin sang out. "Hey, you guys. We got three holes dug already. How about you?"

"We've only just begun," José called from the other end of the orchard. "Wait till we get going. We can dig more than you can any day."

When they started, the air was cool. The weeds were still wet with dew. But the air was getting hotter all the time.

"Hey, Jeff. Come here," Carlos called. "I don't think this is what you want. But look anyhow, will you?"

This time the others kept working while Jeff examined the lump. It turned out to be just another stone.

"We've dug up eight holes already," Kevin yelled after a bit. "Hey, Jeff, I thought you said you'd have something for us to drink. How about getting it?"

Jeff headed for the house, and when he came back, he had plenty of cool lemonade for all.

The García twins turned out to be especially good workers, but they were full of questions.

"Why did the Herrons go down to Colombia in the first place?" Carlos wanted to know when Jeff brought them the lemonade.

"Well, some people live in out-of-the-way places in South America," Jeff began. "In fact, all over the world. Many have their own language. The Herrons wanted to go to one of these groups, live with them, learn their language, and write it down."

"But why?" José asked. "I thought all of South America except Brazil spoke Spanish."

"That's the main language, sure. But lots of Indians live in villages so far from the big cities they never have a chance to learn it. They use their own language instead."

"So after the Herrons learn the Indians' language, what do they do then?" Carlos asked.

"They translate some of the Bible into that language. Then they teach the villagers how to read it."

"Why the Bible? Why not other books?" Carlos asked.

"The Herrons want the Indians to be able to read God's message in the language they really understand," Terry answered.

"But if they never heard it before, what's so important about their hearing it now?" Carlos wondered.

"The really important thing," Jeff said, "is for everyone to hear about Jesus, God's Son. He came to the world to save people from their sins. The Bible tells about it: It says, 'All have sinned.'[1] Then, 'The soul that sinneth, it shall die.'[2] And then, maybe most important, 'For God so loved the world, that He gave His only begotten Son, that whosoever believeth in Him should not perish, but have everlasting life.' "[3]

"I've heard that one," Carlos murmured, "but I've never known what it meant."

"Well, God made the first people," Jeff said. "He told them how He wanted them to live. But they didn't obey. And that was sin. And all of us born since then were born with sin in us too.

"God can't have any sin in heaven. But He does want people to be able to go to heaven to live with Him someday. So He sent His Son, Jesus, to earth to take the punishment—death—for our sin. That's why Jesus died on the cross.

"But each person has to ask Jesus to forgive him and be his Saviour from sin. Then that person can go to heaven when he dies."

Carlos frowned. "Why doesn't everybody ask, if it's all that easy?"

"Some people have never heard," Jeff said. "That's why the Herrons went to Colombia, to give the Guitero Indians a chance to hear God's message from the Bible too."

"And you say they can't go back till they get money to put their son in a special home?" asked José.

"Right. That's why we want to find those opals," Terry answered.

[1] Rom. 3:23
[2] Ezek. 18:4
[3] John 3:16

"Sounds good to me. Come on, José. Let's get digging," said Carlos.

Along about 10:30 everyone took a break. It was plenty hot, so they sat or lay down on the grass in the shade of the big maple tree. The lemonade that trickled down their throats felt cool and tangy.

Mr. and Mrs. Herron came out to thank them. But Mark sat quietly in his wagon, staring blankly.

Just then a car turned in the drive. A young man with a camera got out and walked toward them.

"One of you Jeff Palmer?" he asked.

"I am." Jeff flipped his red hair out of his eyes and got up.

"I'm Tom White from Wycliffe Associates," he explained. "Mrs. Keller phoned and told us about the great Gopher Hole Treasure Hunt. Is it OK if I ask a few questions and take some pictures?"

"Sure. But why?" Jeff wanted to know.

"The people at WA do all they can to help the Wycliffe missionaries," the young man said. "Isn't that just what all of you are doing?"

"They surely are," Mr. Herron called, getting up and shaking the young man's hand. "I'm Jim Herron, the missionary they're helping."

Although he had heard some of the story from Mrs. Keller, Tom wanted to get the story straight from the boys.

"But what are you going to do with the story?" Jeff asked.

"Put it in the WA NEWSLETTER," Tom said. "We have four big stories almost ready for page one. But we might just use yours instead."

"Page one!" Terry exclaimed.

"Why not? This is the kind of story we want. Every-day people helping everyday missionaries in everyday ways. However, I guess not too many people dig up gopher holes every day to help, though, do they?"

"But what if we don't find the marbles?" Jeff wondered. "And what if the Herrons can't go back to Colombia after all? What then?"

"Well, God may supply their needs through your help. He may do it some other way. But you're doing what you can. And that's the story," Tom explained.

"Hey, let's cut out the chatter and get digging," Bill called, heading toward the orchard once more.

"Let's go!" Terry joined in. "We'll find 'em this time for sure."

Camera in hand and film bag over his shoulder, Tom White followed them. Through the weeds and around the mounds he tramped, shooting pictures at every turn. And questions? Jeff figured Tom could write a book with all the answers he got.

Finally Tom pulled a card out of his pocket and gave it to Jeff. "Do me a favor. Phone and tell me how the dig turns out. I've got to rush back, get these films developed, and write up the story. If we can use it in the August issue, we'll need it ready by tomorrow."

"Boy, that's working kind of close, isn't it?" Terry asked.

"We don't plan it that way," Tom told them, "but that's the way it happens once in a while. Let me know the outcome, OK?"

By now the groups were a little more than halfway down the rows of trees. Each would kneel in front of a soft brown mound of dirt. Carefully one person would hold a piece of screening.

The other would scoop up all the loose dirt as far down as he could reach, then dump it on the screen. The other would shake it till most of the dirt fell through. Only the lumps and pebbles would be left.

Of course, that's all they were interested in, the lumps. Some they tried to rub hard against the screen, to see if they were just dirt. Others they could tell were pebbles.

After a lot more digging, Carlos let out a yell. "Jeff, Terry! Come here. I think we've found 'em!"

All the others came running. But someone else came running too. Jeff looked up, Ritter! A frown crossed Jeff's face.

"What are you looking for?" Ritter asked.

"Lumps of yellow clay the missionary kid lost," Bill told him. "Supposed to be real valuable opal in them."

"Hey, that looks like the real thing," Kevin panted as he leaned over Bill's shoulder.

Jeff tried to shut his ears to all the babble as he examined the pieces. Yes, they sure seemed to be the lumps all right. A little darker yellow than he'd remembered.

"Hey, Terry, get Mr. Herron, will you? He'll know for sure."

Before Jeff even finished, Terry had dashed away.

"How many did you find?" Jeff asked.

"Four," Carlos told him.

"There should be six," Jeff said. And before he got the words out, José began digging again, deep down in the hole.

"Hey, here's another," Carlos exploded, as one rolled down the screen he was holding.

"Keep digging!" Jeff encouraged.

"Give us room, will you?" José growled at the others.

Grudgingly, they backed up a bit. But still José bumped into them every time he moved. Soon he held up a sixth lump and they all cheered.

In another moment Mr. Herron was hurrying their way. "You've really been digging up a storm!"

"Yeah!" Bill glanced around, his hands on his hips. "Looks like a tortured orchard!" Everyone laughed.

"What have you found?" Mr. Herron asked.

"I'm not sure," Jeff said.

Mr. Herron stooped down and studied the pieces. "They're sure the right size," he murmured. "A little darker, though. Maybe that's because they got damp being buried so long."

The missionary studied them a bit more. Then he frowned. "I just can't be sure."

"Think Uncle Marv could tell?" Jeff asked.

"Why don't you phone him?" suggested Terry.

Jeff headed for the house as if a bear were chasing him. In a few minutes he was back, puffing like crazy. "He'll be over in a few minutes," he panted. "By the way, Mrs. Keller says it's time to eat. And you should smell the food!"

A big grin spread across Kevin's face. "Let's go!" he cried.

Jeff lagged behind the others and watched as Ritter squinted at the holes that had been dug.

"Still got plenty to dig if they're not the right lumps," Ritter remarked.

"I think they are," Jeff said, as he moved away. But he was worried. If they *weren't* the ones, Ritter might find the real ones while they were eating lunch. "Why don't you come have lunch with us?" Jeff called to Ritter.

Ritter laughed. "Afraid I'll find the real clay lumps?" he asked sarcastically. "No, thanks, I'll stay out here."

When they had all lined up at the picnic table, Mr. Herron asked the blessing. Then the group began to fill their plates.

"One hundred and seventy eight holes?" Mr. Herron gasped. "You kids sure have done a lot of digging!"

"But what if they aren't the right lumps?" Jeff fretted.

"You tried," Mrs. Keller reminded him, "and that's what counts. Now fill your plates. When you finish, come back for seconds. That's an order!"

Carlos grinned. "You won't have to tell us that twice."

Before some of them had a chance for seconds, Uncle Marv drove up in his old pickup. Jeff ran over to help him.

"We found 'em, Uncle Marv," Jeff said excitedly. "At least, I think we did."

The man put his arms through the leather-lined rings of his crutches and gripped the handles firmly. "Well, what are you waiting for? Show them to me."

Everyone bunched around as Uncle Marv examined the lumps at the picnic table. Carefully he pulled the jeweler's loop out of his shirt pocket. It was a strong magnifying glass he always had on a leather cord ound his neck.

"Are they the right ones?" Terry wanted to know.

Uncle Marv looked up, a twinkle in his eyes. "If you guys would give me half a chance." He laughed and reached in his pocket for a knife.

Carefully he scraped away some of the clay. It came off easily. Too easily, Jeff thought, as he peered down.

"Well," Uncle Marv said, frowning, "this one sure isn't anything to write home about." Then he picked up another.

"Oh, no," Jeff moaned.

"Don't worry," Carlos said. "He's still got five to go."

Uncle Marv went on scraping and gently tapping each piece. "Are you sure these are the lumps Mark brought home?"

"They look like them," Mr. Herron said. "I wondered if they had changed color because of getting damp."

"Could be," answered Uncle Marv.

In a few minutes the group grew quiet. Not one lump had anything in it yet.

"There's still one left," Terry tried to sound cheerful. "And it's the biggest."

Uncle Marv worked on in silence. In a minute they had the answer: just another hunk of yellow sandstone.

Slowly the group moved away, sitting back down to finish the meal. But right then Jeff didn't feel like eating. He'd been so sure the marbles would be in the orchard—.

For a moment Jeff just stood looking. Suddenly, he spotted a flash of light. It came from the bushes between his place and Ritter's.

A reflection, that's what it was, of Ritter's field glasses. He was spying on them again.

Well, right now Jeff really didn't care. No one would have to tell Ritter. By the way they all looked, anyone could tell they hadn't found the real clay marbles.

With an ache inside, Jeff glanced around the lawn. He looked at the group that had spent the morning working so hard in the hot sun. Then he looked at the Herrons, God's workers from Colombia. That's where his parents should have been right now—where he should have been.

Then Jeff looked at Mark. Why had God allowed Mark's accident in the first place? And if that had to be, why had God allowed Mark to lose those valuable clay lumps? Why hadn't God answered all their prayers and let them find the marbles? *Why?*

Suddenly Jeff felt very angry inside. He just couldn't understand any of it.

Chapter 6

Lost and Found

It was a mighty discouraged boy who trudged upstairs to his bedroom that night. He didn't even bother to switch on the light. As he started to take off his clothes, he moved silently toward the window. Very little cool air blew in. By morning his room would be comfortable. But now, the air still felt hot and sticky.

Suddenly Jeff saw a flash of light out past the barn. Just a flicker, then it was gone. Jeff watched for a while. Then he saw it again. Someone was out there with a flashlight. But who could it be? Ritter? Surely not at this time of night!

For a long while Jeff kept looking. But the light seemed to have vanished. Maybe he had only imagined it. Maybe he hadn't seen a light after all.

Soon he shrugged, climbed into bed, and drifted off to sleep.

The next morning both Jeff and Terry had chores to do. Along with other things, Jeff cut and trimmed the huge front yard. Then he fed and watered his worms.

It was 11 o'clock when Terry finally came over. The boys again took care of Mark so the Herrons could get some work done.

It was then that Jeff remembered. "Hey, Terry, I saw a light back in the orchard last night. At least, I think I did."

"Oh, come on, Jeff. What would anyone be doing back there?"

"Don't know—unless it was Ritter. Let's go look."

They took Mark with them. When they got there, they knew right away something was different.

"Didn't we stop digging right about here?" Terry asked.

"Yeah. It was near this tree that Carlos found the lumps," answered Jeff. "This one with the broken limb."

"But," Terry just looked in amazement, "we only dug to here. Now everything's dug up."

"I'll bet it *was* Ritter," Jeff said angrily.

"If he found those lumps, we'll never see them again," Terry said with a frown.

"That's for sure," Jeff agreed.

Trudging back, Jeff started mumbling, "Boy, how do you love a guy like that?"

"What 'cha mean, Jeff?"

"I mean, the Bible says to love our enemies. You know, act pleasant to them. Respect them. Be nice to them. But how can I feel that way toward Ritter?"

Soon the boys were sprawled in the shade of the huge maple tree between the house and the barn. For a while they just lay there and thought. Even Mark wrinkled up his forehead and looked as if he were thinking.

Suddenly, Jeff rolled over. "Mark, where did you put those marbles? The marbles. Know what I mean?"

Mark glanced towards the bird feeder.

Jeff sighed. "He doesn't understand. He thinks I'm talking about the birds."

"Marbles!" Mark said it clearly.

Jeff flipped over. "Yes! Marbles. What . . . did . . . you . . . do . . . with the marbles?"

"Marbles . . . bird . . . feeder?" Mark said slowly.

"Oh, man," Jeff groaned. "See what I mean? He just doesn't . . ."

Terry jumped up. "The bird feeder! We never looked there!"

Jeff sprang to his feet. Together they dashed to the board hanging from one of the limbs.

Reaching high over their heads, they felt around in the cans nailed to the feeder.

"I've got one!" Terry yelled.

"So have I," shouted Jeff. "Hey, we've finally found 'em!"

They added them up. There were five.

"Mine!" Mark yelled as he saw the marbles in their hands. "Marbles mine!"

The boys tried to keep them away, but Mark whimpered louder.

"All right, all right," Jeff growled impatiently. "At least we found them."

Quickly he tore over to the apartment, where the Herrons had returned a short time earlier, and shouted out the news.

"Mark told us where they were," Jeff explained. "Hey that's *right*. Mark *told* us!"

Terry grinned. "Mark said, 'Marbles, bird feeder.' "

"Well, praise the Lord!" said Mrs. Herron, wiping

away a tear. "He's starting to understand things again, thanks to you boys. You're a real answer to prayer. You've helped him so much."

Jeff glanced away, embarrassed. He'd never thought of himself as an answer to anyone's prayers. But it did make him feel good inside to hear Mrs. Herron say it.

"How are we going to get them away from him?" Jeff wondered.

"Find something else he wants," the missionary suggested. "Then try to swap."

From then till lunch, the boys tried. First one treasure then another. But nothing worked.

"Well, I don't like to do it," Mr. Herron said, "but I guess we must. I'll go downtown and buy a bunch of regular marbles. Then when Mark takes his nap, I'll fill the leather pouch with the new ones."

After lunch, the boys waited impatiently. Mark was resting. But for a long while he just wouldn't go to sleep. When he did, Mr. Herron swapped the marbles and came back outside.

Mr. Herron made it plenty clear that he didn't think this was going to turn out to be the big miracle as the boys thought it would be. Still, he looked more hopeful as all three of them got in the car and hurried to Uncle Marv's.

Jeff and Terry could hardly wait to tell him. At last they had found the real things: the clay lumps, all the way from Lightning Ridge, Australia. And they'd be full of opal, the boys were sure. Worth plenty too. This would be the answer they'd been praying for.

"Uncle Marv?" Jeff called when they couldn't find him anywhere. "Hey, Uncle Marv, where are you?"

His pickup was there. His garage-shop door was open. But no Uncle Marv.

Just then a car eased into the drive.

"Aunt Flo!" Jeff shouted. "Uncle Marv!" Jeff opened the door on his uncle's side.

"What happened?" Terry gasped. Uncle Marv's hands were hidden, wrapped in soft, bulging bandages.

"Get my wheelchair, would you please?" Uncle Marv asked.

"But what happened?" Jeff asked again.

"The furnace in the shop exploded when I went to light it," he explained. "Gas leak, I guess."

"Why didn't you call us?" Mr. Herron asked. "We would have been glad to help."

"I didn't want to worry Matty. She has enough troubles already." Then he grinned at Jeff. "Hey, fella, am I going to grow roots here in this car, or are you going to get me my winged chariot?"

Jeff and Terry both dashed off. When they got back, Jeff frowned as he said, "We just found the real clay lumps. We were hoping you would grind them for us."

The crippled man said nothing while Mr. Herron helped him slide from the car into his wheelchair.

"Well, if you want me to grind them, you'll have to wait. The doc said these bandages can come off in a week or two."

"A week?" said Jeff.

"Well, I've been teaching you to grind for months now," answered Uncle Marv. "Why don't you grind them?"

"Me?" Jeff gasped. "I'm just beginning to learn how to grind agates and jaspers. They're real common gemstones. You want *me* to grind valuable black opal?"

"Don't worry," Uncle Marv chuckled. "I'll be right there watching you. Come on, start pushing me over to the shop, will you?"

"But," Jeff felt weak at the thought of grinding such a valuable gem.

"You just have to go slower and be gentler. Besides, I'll let you start them. If there's anything good inside, I'll finish them up when I can."

Before they all headed for the barn, Mr. Herron promised Aunt Flo that he'd stay with Uncle Marv till she could straighten things out at work. She would arrange for a few days off to care for him.

A few minutes later, after Aunt Flo left, Jeff was sitting in front of the 220 grit grinding wheel at his uncle's workbench.

"First turn the machine on," the man instructed. "Then the water. Be sure a small, steady stream flows on the wheel at all times.

"Now take one of the lumps. Get a firm grip on it. Then move it slowly, very slowly, until it just touches the wheel."

Jeff felt himself shaking as he reached toward the spinning wheel.

"STOP!" Uncle Marv yelled.

Jeff jumped. The lump shot right out of his hand and plunked into the water tray beneath the whirling wheel.

"Hey, Jeff boy, you're not trying to jam a dull spear through the hide of a 100-year-old hippo! Touch it lightly. Now turn off the machine. When the wheel stops, pick up the lump and start over."

"Uncle Marv, why don't we just wait till you get well?" pleaded Jeff.

Uncle Marv looked at Jeff for a moment. Then he said, "Jeff, you've got to build confidence in your own abilities sometime. Why not start now?"

Again Jeff gripped the clay lump. Then, bracing his arms on the table, he moved his fingers ever so slightly toward the spinning wheel.

"Slowly, slowly," said Uncle Marv.

"If he moves much more slowly," Terry quipped, "he'll be going backwards!"

Jeff pulled his hands away. They were shaking hard.

"Uncle Marv, why don't we wait?" he asked again.

The man in the wheelchair spoke softly this time. "Jeff, you and Terry have worked long and prayed hard to locate these chunks of clay. Now you have them, do you mean to tell me you want to wait another seven days to find out if they have opal in them?"

Jeff sighed. Again he picked up the lump and carefully moved it forward. A small trail of yellow formed on the spinning wheel as it bit into the clay.

"Hold it! You're doing fine," encouraged Uncle Marv. "Now take the loop off my neck. That's my jeweler's magnifying glass, you know. Put it around your neck. Now dry off the lump and look through the loop. See if there's the slightest hint of black where you've ground."

Carefully Jeff studied the piece. No, there wasn't a speck of any color but yellow. He even let the others look.

"What you've got to do," Uncle Marv explained, "is grind away a fraction at a time. The second you get to black, if you get to it at all, stop! That black is opal."

Black opal! Jeff shivered with excitement. Uncle Marv had said it was one of the most expensive gemstones in the world.

Carefully, Jeff held the lump up. Ever so slowly he pressed it against the wheel. He took it off and looked. Still no black.

Again and again, he shaved off paper-thin bits. But no black.

"Oh, man," Terry groaned. "You don't have enough left to grind.

Jeff looked at the tiny flake of clay left in his fingers. Then he sat back. He felt weak, as if he had just run all the way to the swimming pool and back without stopping.

"OK, Jeff. Remember I told you perhaps one in a thousand of those lumps just might contain opal? That's why it's so valuable. Now take the next piece. Grind it the same way."

Jeff frowned at the four lumps left on the table. Before, he had been so sure they would be the answer to the Herrons' problems. But now? He almost hated to try another.

Carefully, Jeff brought the second lump to the spinning wheel. Again it made a trail of yellow, and again he pulled it away, dried it off, and looked. But even using Uncle Marv's 10-power loop, he saw no hint of black.

The first, the second, and the third lumps were all the same. Nothing but clay. On to the fourth. The wheel bit into it just slightly. Jeff examined it.

"Uncle Marv! Look!" Jeff was shaking so hard that

Mr. Herron had to hold the loop up to the other man's eyes.

"It's black, all right. But it's so small. Grind right beside it. Just a bit. If it is opal, we don't want to loose a flake of it."

Jeff had to lean his elbows on the table again so his shaking hand would hold the stone still. Again, he pulled the lump away, dried it off, and looked.

Then, for a long moment, Uncle Marv examined the piece. When he straightened up, he was all smiles. "Jeff, I think you've found something!"

Jeff felt a mile tall. He just sat there and grinned.

"Better put that to one side. I'll finish it next week."

"That's fine with me!" Jeff sounded as if he'd just gotten out of chores for a week.

Again, with the fifth lump, Jeff ground and ground. After a bit, there was nothing left to grind but his fingertips. Turning the machine off, he dried his hands. "Well, anyhow. We got one out of five."

"What do you think it's worth?" Terry asked.

"Can't tell till we weigh it. Have to go in the house for that," said Uncle Marv.

Inside, Mr. Herron helped Uncle Marv weigh the lump on the jeweler's balance. Quickly Uncle Marv figured what the piece might weigh when it was completely cleaned up and polished.

"Well," he said slowly, "I'd guess perhaps it will yield four to six carats of gem quality black opal."

"A carat? What's that?" Terry asked.

"A carat is a jeweler's weight," Uncle Marv explained. "It weighs about as much as a whisper."

"Aw, come on," Terry said. "How much is that?"

"All right, I'll tell you. An American penny weighs about 15 carats."

"Oh, man! That'll only weigh four carats?" Jeff moaned. "We won't get anything for that."

Uncle Marv raised his bushy eyebrows. "Jeff, top quality black opal can retail for as much as $3,000 per carat. And from what I can see, this piece is top quality."

A wide grin spread over Terry's face. "Hey, great! Now all we've got to do is find the sixth one. Then we'll have it made."

"Wait, Jeff," Mr. Herron said. "Remember, Uncle Marv said retail. We'd be lucky to get half of that."

"I'd say we could sell it for between $2,000 and $8,000." said Uncle Marv.

Jeff squinted at the small lump. Two thousand for that? Wow! That was plenty. But still not enough to pay for a home for Mark while the Herrons went back.

"We've got to find the sixth one," he told Terry. "That was bigger. Maybe it'll be better too."

Chapter 7

Problems

Back at the farm, everyone was pleased about the opal. But what about the sixth lump? It was larger. Shouldn't it be even better than the rest?

While the boys had been away, Mrs. Herron had watched Mark. She had let him wander all over. Fortunately, he had not missed the clay marbles.

Then while the Herrons wrote some letters in their apartment, Jeff and Terry took over. It was hot. Mark moved slowly. Finally he settled down in his wagon. Carefully he dumped his marbles out and pushed them around. He even tried to shoot one.

"I've never seen him do that before," Jeff said. "He's really getting better. Let's watch."

"Look!" Jeff whispered when they got there.

Mixed up with all the bright colored glassies was the sixth clay marble. Mark must have found it in his wanderings while they were at Uncle Marv's.

Jeff and Terry were plenty excited as Mr. Herron drove them over to Uncle Marv's again. But the excitement faded like smoke in the wind when they found the lump was only clay.

A lot happened the next three weeks. Jeff sold some

worms to a man who rented boats at a lake nearby. Uncle Marv gave Jeff a few more lessons in grinding the beautiful jasper from Rainbow Ridge. And Jeff and Terry went with Uncle Marv down to the center of Los Angeles to the Jewelry Mart. It was a large building full of little shops. They went from dealer to dealer, trying to sell the black opal.

Everyone liked it, but few wanted to pay what it was worth. Finally someone did give Uncle Marv a check for $4,000, its wholesale price.

Jeff knew the Herrons would be thankful. It would be a start toward paying for Mark's three years in the States. But somehow Jeff felt pain inside. What was only $4,000 when they needed $24,000?

In that three weeks, a letter came from the County Home for Retarded Children. They would not be able to take care of Mark for the next three years. The Herrons had not lived in the county long enough.

Another letter came from Wycliffe headquarters in Colombia asking if the Herrons would be coming back in mid-September to teach. They wanted them badly. But if they couldn't come, Wycliffe would need to know so they could get someone else.

Jeff and Terry listened as Mr. Herron read the letters aloud. And when he finished, he frowned.

"Jim," Mrs. Herron said, reaching for her husband's hand, "we have a job to finish out there. Maybe we'd better plan to go and have faith that the Lord will work things out for our Mark."

"But we're not leaving him!" Mr. Herron answered. Jeff thought the man's voice sounded a little too loud, a little too harsh. "If the Lord had wanted us to go,

He would have provided. The county home won't take him, and the $4,000 from the opal is not the $24,000 we need for the private home."

"Is that really the problem?" his wife asked gently. "Neither of us wants to go back without him, do we? You know how much I love our only son too."

Jeff and Terry watched the two missionaries. Mr. Herron looked deeply troubled. "But it's not fair," he said. "First Mark is badly hurt. And now God is asking us to take off and leave him."

"He's alive," Mrs. Herron replied, "and he's improving. Maybe it's time we accepted God's will about Mark," she said quietly. "No matter what, God knows best."

Jeff thought that watching Mr. Herron's face was like watching a summer sky. First came the thunderheads, the lightning, the rain. Then, gradually, the showers lightened, and the storm was over.

"Come over here, Mark," Mr. Herron said. "Sit here between your mother and me."

He bowed his head and so did Terry and Jeff. "Dear Lord," he prayed. "Thank You for Your goodness to us. Thank You for giving us our son, Mark. Thank You for the years of good health he's had. And thank You that he's getting better every day.

"Now, Lord, You know we don't want to leave him home. But if we must, help us—help me to make Your will my will. Make me willing to obey, no matter what. In Jesus' holy name we pray, Amen."

Jeff looked up. Again he studied Mr. Herron's face. The "storm" was over. The "sun" was shining through.

Mrs. Herron kissed her husband and Mark. Then

she said, "We'll have to buy some new clothes for three years in the jungle. When shall I start?"

For a long moment the missionary looked at his wife. Then he said softly, "Any time, Dear."

Again Jeff felt as if a giant fist were gripping his stomach. The Herrons just had to have that money for Mark. And somehow, some way, Jeff had to help them get it.

In that same three weeks, something else happened. The Wycliffe Associates NEWSLETTER for August came out. The front-page story was "The Great Gopher Hole Treasure Hunt."

WA had sent enough copies for Jeff and Terry to give one to each of those who had helped in the "hunt." Besides that, thousands of other copies had been sent all over the United States.

After the boys had delivered the extra copies, they sprawled out in the shade of the giant maple. There they read the story for the umpteenth time.

Terry grinned. "It talks about our being on the Herrons' missionary team. How do you like that?"

"Yeah," Jeff murmured. But the awful hurt was building up inside him again.

Terry looked at his friend. "What's the matter, Jeff?"

"In a way, it's a story of failure. First we failed to find the marbles. Then, when we did, they weren't worth enough."

"Hey, Jeff, you're talking like that monkey is still on your back. That old guilt feeling about your parents' accident. I thought I told you . . . "

"I still have nightmares," said Jeff.

"Man, you're in a bad way."

"Yeah. But we've just got to do something." Suddenly Jeff jumped up and ran to the apartment. Terry followed.

"Mr. Herron," Jeff said, when the missionary came to the door, "you've got $4,000, and you need $24,000. Right?

"That leaves $20,000 to go," said Mr. Herron sadly.

"I've got $20,000," said Jeff. "I want to give it to you. Then Mark can get the help he needs here."

Mr. Herron looked surprised. For a moment he didn't know what to say. But he pushed open the screen door and motioned for the boys to come in.

"It's his dad's life insurance," Terry said.

"Jeff, we appreciate your generosity. But we could never accept it. Your dad meant for that to take care of you—for your college education, maybe."

Jeff looked as if he were about to cry, but the missionary put his arm on Jeff's shoulder. "If the Lord wants to send in the money, He'll do it. He's been teaching me that these past few weeks. And we can trust Him to do it in a way that will be right for everyone."

They talked a while longer. Then the boys went out to wait for Mark. Soon Jeff had another idea. "Terry, what about going up the East Fork? I hear there's still plenty of gold up there in Dead Man's Mine. Problem is, people just can't seem to find it. Maybe if we took flashlights and went way back in, we just might be able to find a new vein."

"Hey, Jeff. Now you're *really* dreaming," said Terry, shaking his head.

Jeff went on as if he'd never heard. "I've read about mines. Lots of times a person starts a hole. He spends all his money, digs as far as he can, doesn't find a thing, so he quits. Later some other guy comes along, takes a few swings with his pick, and discovers a real rich vein."

"Jeff, you don't only have nightmares, now you're beginning to have day-mares, too!"

"Well, we can try, can't we?" Jeff argued.

Although Terry felt they were only kidding themselves, he finally agreed to take Jeff up the mountain to the mine early the next morning.

Chapter 8

Search for Gold

Early the next morning Jeff and Terry got ready. The boys felt they should take five things: flashlights with new batteries, army picks (the kind with the short handles), two canteens of water, a couple of rock sacks, and plastic shields to protect their eyes.

Starting about 8 o'clock, they got to the mountains by nine. A little way beyond the end of the dirt road they hid their bikes under some bushes.

For a while the trail followed a dry creek bed. It started out easy enough. But before long, the way grew steep. Once a long time ago there had been a jeep trail up to the mine. Some of the way it had followed the creek, snaking its way back and forth across the creek many times. But since an earthquake, the creek bed was filled with boulders that had rolled off the hillsides. No jeep could possibly make it now. Even the jeep trail was strewn with rocks. The boys were always having to step around them, and, sometimes, even over them.

"Hey, man," Jeff groaned, slumping down on a flat rock beside the trail. "Slow down, will you? I'm pooped."

Terry grinned. But he, too, was glad for a break. "We sure picked a hot day, didn't we?"

For a bit they just sat and puffed. Then Jeff started gulping water from his canteen.

"Hey, knock that off!" Terry snapped. "You'll be sick drinking so much after climbing that hard."

Jeff lowered his canteen. "Great! I'm dying of thirst. And I can't even take a swig."

"Not too much," Terry corrected, "and not too fast. You'll bring up your breakfast."

Jeff screwed the cap back on and slipped his canteen into his rock sack. "How much farther?"

Terry glanced upward. "Half, three quarters of an hour more."

Jeff frowned. "Been up there much?"

"Plenty of times with the scouts. We even found gold once."

Jeff jumped up ready to go. "Where?"

Terry picked up his sack, heavy with tools. "The big tunnel goes straight in. Then two tunnels branch to the right. And four to the left."

"So, where did you find the gold?" repeated Jeff.

"Oh, yeah. Third tunnel on the left," answered Terry.

Jeff started out fast. "What are we waiting for?"

"Man, I still say you're dreaming." Terry shook his head. "No way is there any gold left in that mine."

Jeff whirled around. "And where are we going to get the money for Herrons then?"

"Hey, man. God doesn't ask you to do the impossible, you know. Finding lost marbles. Sure. We can do that. But digging up $20,000 worth of gold? No way, man. No way."

After a while they could see the entrance to Dead Man's Mine high above them. It was in the side of the cliff.

From the level spot at the bottom of the slope, they gazed upward. Much of what had been dug out of the mine had made a landslide down the hill.

"Third tunnel on the left?" Jeff asked as he started. "Let's go."

It was bad enough that they had to crawl on their hands and knees. But with the noonday sun glaring down on them, they actually felt faint.

Finally they scrambled up to the tiny level spot in front of the mine. For a while all they did was lie on the ground and catch their breath.

The miners had built a retaining wall of rocks to support the level spot. Then they had shoveled dirt out of the mine on top of the rocks.

Jeff looked around. A huge boulder, about three feet across, balanced on the edge. One good shove, he thought, and it would go crashing down. But it was much too hot to do anything they didn't have to do.

After a bit, Jeff crawled to the edge. "Man, is that steep!" he gasped. "I sure wouldn't want to slide down there."

Moving back toward Terry again, he noticed a weathered post with a bit of wood nailed to the top. "Wonder what that sign said."

Terry squinted. "Maybe 'Private! Keep Out!' Guess we'll never know. Hey, it'll be cooler inside. Let's go."

Although neither of them felt as if he could move another millimeter, they crawled into the shade of the tunnel. The cooler air inside felt good.

"Look at that wood," Jeff said, studying the heavy beams on the sides and top of the tunnel.

"Railroad ties. That's what you call shoring. All these San Gabriel Mountains are made up of decomposed granite. Mostly it's broken up chunks of rock. They need that shoring for safety."

"Third one to the left!" Jeff said, standing up. "Watch your head. It's kind of low in here."

For quite a while, the light coming in the entrance enabled them to see. But the farther they crawled in, the darker it got.

"Here it is," Jeff yelled, snapping his light on. While the main tunnel had been long, this one was short. Jeff's light reached the end, about 15 feet away.

"No shoring here. Hope we don't have an earthquake today."

Quickly they chose a place to start. Both boys put on their eye shields. Then Jeff knelt down, pulled out his pick, and started swinging. He hit the wall about at eye level. The steel of the pick rang as it struck the white quartz. A small chunk of dirt-covered rock fell out.

Jeff held his light close. "Hey, Terry. In the crack. Look."

"Gold!" Terry yelled. "Hey, man. That's what we're looking for. Gold! Here, let me dig."

Taking tiny chips with his pick, he dug all around it. Finally the chunk of white rock fell into Jeff's waiting hands.

"Gold!" Jeff grinned at the tiny crack of yellow. "Real gold. And I'll bet there's plenty more behind that. Let's get going."

Feverishly, they started widening the hole. After a bit, kneeling on their rock sacks began to hurt. So they squatted on their heels and picked away. Loose dirt and rock piled up around their knees. Every now and then they had to push it away, so they'd have enough room to work.

"Didn't I tell you we'd find gold?" Jeff cheered as he chopped away. "Remember, I told you how lots of miners quit just before they found it? Then someone comes along later and strikes it rich."

Terry sat back on his feet, puffing. "Sure. We found one piece. But . . . "

"Aw. Don't be a wet blanket. We'll find more; I know."

Swinging their picks was hard work. The boys found little energy left to talk. Finally Terry struggled to his feet. "Oh, my legs!"

"Mine too. You know, there must be an easier way to get gold," said Jeff.

"There is," Terry told him. "Ever heard of panning? All you do is get a big flat pan, like a pie tin. Then you find a stream. In gold country, of course."

"Is this gold country?" Jeff asked.

"Not like northern California. But some people still pan in the streams here," Terry answered.

"But what do you do with the pan?" asked Jeff.

Terry grinned. "Well, you get your pan full of sand and water. Then swish it around and around. The sand will wash out over the edges. The gold will stay at the bottom."

"That sounds easy enough. Maybe we should try that," Jeff said.

"Slow down, old buddy. Nothing's ever as easy as it sounds. Nothing."

"Hey, let's stop talking and open up this vein," Jeff sank to his knees again. "We can go panning later."

Terry looked down at his friend in the darkness of the tunnel and shook his head. Then he got to work too.

"Oh, man. My arms ache," Terry groaned, after some more pick swinging. "Don't yours?"

"Sure." Jeff smashed his pick into the wall again. "But we've got to get some more gold."

"I still say we're crazy," Terry complained.

"Yea. Crazy like a fox when we hit that vein," Jeff retorted.

Once again they stopped briefly for a drink from their canteens. After a while their flashlights began to fade, but they kept working. Soon Jeff's light went out. "Oh, no. We just about had it, and our lights give out!" he groaned.

Terry snapped off his fading flashlight and rested in the darkness. "That's what they all say, my friend. 'If only my money had held out,' or 'If only my food had held out,' or 'If only my light had held out, I would have struck it rich!'"

Jeff felt like saying something, but he clamped his mouth shut. Terry was probably right. He always seemed to be. But why? *Why* couldn't they have been the lucky ones to find gold? Why?

"Well, we tried, anyhow," Terry said, trying to encourage his friend.

"Know what we forgot? Lunch." Terry reached for his canteen. "No way will water ever replace food."

Slowly the boys worked their way back to the main tunnel and out. Jeff got to the entrance first.

"Oh," he groaned, squeezing his eyes shut. "I can't see."

"Stop!" Terry yelled. "You might fall."

Jeff sank down to his knees and covered his eyes. Slowly he parted his fingers until he got used to the brightness.

"Man, is it hot!" Terry murmured as he too slumped down.

Hot, hungry, and tired, they headed down the many switchbacks to the flat area below. Sometimes they seemed to turn right back on themselves. The trail was more like a snake, winding back and forth, first one way, then the other, till it reached the plateau far below.

Not many people used those trails during the summer heat. Most were closed because of fire hazard. So the boys were surprised when three men came struggling toward them. Each carried a new flight bag from a foreign airline.

Terry looked longingly at the bags. "You guys are smart, bringing your lunch."

At first they looked startled. Then the tall one with the mustache laughed. "What's the matter, fellas? Forget you had to eat once in a while?"

The other two just glared as they passed. Especially the heavy man with the wrinkled, baggy pants and the torn tennis shoes.

The boys moved on in silence till they got around a bend in the trail.

"Those guys never were scouts," Terry whispered.

"How do you know?"

"See those old sneakers that big guy had on? Any scout knows you don't hike in those. For one thing, you can feel sharp rocks right through the bottoms. That can really bug you."

"They sure weren't friendly," Jeff said. "Let's hurry. I'm starved."

At the end of the dirt road they found a parked car. "Must belong to those guys," Jeff mused. "I'm going to copy down their license number. 'DRP 479.' "

Terry gave him a quizzical look. "Why do that?"

"Something strange about those guys. I just don't know," answered Jeff.

"Oh, Jeff, you're always trying to play detective!"

Back home after a late lunch, the boys went over to the apartment.

"See what we found?" Jeff showed the missionary the white rock with the gold in it. "Up in Dead Man's Mine."

"You fellows starting a mineral collection?" asked Mr. Herron.

"We wanted to find $20,000 worth," said Jeff sadly.

The man grinned. "Just a bit short, aren't you?"

Just then the bush between the yards parted. Out stepped Ritter, field glasses strung around his neck as usual. "Mind if I see?" he asked.

"Oh, no!" Jeff groaned as he held out the precious rock.

"By the way," Mr. Herron told them. "While you were gone, it seems a few other fellows felt short of money. Only they thought they'd get it the easy way."

"Yeah? What did they do?" asked Terry.

"Robbed a bank. Got away with about $50,000, I heard," said Mr. Herron.

"You see 'em?" Terry wondered.

The man laughed. "No, and I'm just as glad. But I heard it on the news at noon."

Just then Mrs. Herron called. "Phone for you, Jim." When Mr. Herron had left, Ritter left too, and the boys were plenty glad.

Left alone, they both were deep in thought. Finally Jeff looked up. "Are you thinking what I'm thinking?"

"Those three guys?" asked Terry.

"I'll bet they're the ones. I'll bet they were carrying the money in those flight bags." Jeff got talking faster and faster, like a boulder rolling down a hill. "They went up to hide the money in the mine. No one goes up there this time of year."

Terry grinned. "No one in his right mind, you mean."

"What do you say we go back?" Jeff urged. "Find the money and get a reward."

"Oh, sure, and if those guys catch us, we'll get a lot more than a reward," warned Terry.

"Hey, we can wait till tomorrow," Jeff said. "They'll be gone for sure, then."

"Jeff, that monkey on your back sure gives your mind a weird twist. Just because we see three guys climbing up a lonely trail, you figure they're bank robbers. You're crazy, you know!"

"Oh, yeah? You said yourself they weren't dressed for hiking. Look at those beat-up old sneakers that one guy had on. Was he planning to hike?"

Terry frowned. "You've got something there."

"Well, I'm going back. If you want to come, fine,"

said Jeff. "If you don't, well, I'm going anyhow."

Terry shook his head. "OK, you win. No way will I let you go back alone. How about tomorrow afternoon? I've got to do my four hours' work in the morning."

Jeff grinned. "I knew you'd go."

Chapter 9

Unexpected Help

The next morning Mr. Herron wanted to take the boys to Wycliffe Headquarters with him. So he phoned Terry's mom to ask if he could skip work. She said yes.

On their way he explained. "Their new office building is done. Now they're finishing up an apartment complex. It'll be for the missionaries to live in when they have to stay just a short time."

"You say the apartments are ready?" Jeff asked.

"Not quite. They're painting them now."

"Painting." Terry laughed. "That's one thing I'm good at. We wouldn't mind helping."

"Remember the time you painted your barn?" Jeff kidded. "I told you that we were opposites. Your face was brown with white paint spots all over. And my face was white with brown freckle spots all over."

Terry grinned. "I sure splashed a lot that day."

When they arrived, Mr. Herron showed them around the offices, the library, the film room, and then took them over to the new building.

"I've got a couple of willing helpers for you," he told the man in charge. "They say they're experts."

"Boy, we sure can use a couple of experts around here," the man joked. "OK, fellows. Why don't you try the third door down the hall. The man in there can get you started."

Jeff and Terry introduced themselves to the short, white-haired man in overalls. "Just call me Walt," the man said, mixing up another can of paint. "You can use these brushes."

For a while they painted in silence as they got used to the feel of the brushes and the thickness of the paint. Then Jeff spoke up. "Boy, was I ever wrong!"

"What do you mean, 'wrong'?" asked Terry.

"About missionaries. I used to think that all they had to do was to ask God for something and right away God would answer their prayers with a yes."

"Yeah," Terry broke in, "and you figured that the missionaries never had any real hard problems. God always took care of them."

Jeff frowned. "Was I ever wrong!"

"Wrong?" asked the little man across the room. "What do you mean?"

Quickly, the boys told him about Mark's accident and the money the Herrons needed to put him in a home.

"I wish they'd taken Mark at the County Home," Jeff said. "With all the doctors they've got there, I'll bet one of them could cure Mark a little faster."

"Have they taken the boy to a specialist?" asked the man.

"Yes, but maybe a different one could help more," Jeff said.

"Well," the old man began slowly, "God may still

provide the money or some other means as a 'Yes' answer. God doesn't always work the way *we* think He should."

"He doesn't always work miracles, either," Terry added.

"Miracles?" questioned the man.

Jeff told him all about the clay lumps. "God could have provided the whole $24,000 just by letting all those marbles turn out to be opals. That would have been some kind of miracle, wouldn't it?"

Walt put his paintbrush down. "Are you the boys who dug up all those gopher holes? The ones they wrote about in the NEWSLETTER?"

The boys grinned. "Yeah. That's us."

"Say, isn't that great! That story did a lot for me, and for a lot of other people too, I'm sure," Walt told them.

"I don't get it," Terry said. "How did our story do anything for you?"

"It helped my wife and me decide to volunteer for short-term missionary work. We're going to New Guinea for a while."

"Just because of that story?" asked Terry.

"Because of what the story said you did," Walt corrected. "You did what you could for God. And as we read it, God asked my wife and me if we were willing to do all we could for Him."

"Hey, that's great!" Terry grinned so wide it looked as if his face might split.

Jeff got a warm feeling inside. Maybe the hunt hadn't been a complete failure after all. God had used it to help others, if not the Herrons.

After a couple of hours Jeff put down his paint-brush. "Is my arm ever tired!"

"These brushes are plenty heavy," Terry said. "The ones I use at home are a lot smaller." ·

Just then the man in charge strode into the room. "OK, Dr. Walt, why don't you and the boys clean up. It's almost time for the 11:30 prayer meeting."

Jeff frowned. "Dr. Walt?"

"That's right, Dr. Walter Willoughby, Psychiatrist."

"But a doctor—painting?" questioned Jeff.

"Even doctors have to work once in a while," the doctor said, laughing. "I'm retired now. We live with my son in Nebraska."

"A psychiatrist?" Jeff wondered. "Isn't that a brain doctor? Would you try to cure Mark?"

The white-haired man put some paint thinner on a rag and started cleaning his hands. "Haven't they already taken him to a specialist?" he asked.

"Yes, but maybe you know something he doesn't. Maybe you could cure him faster. It wouldn't hurt to find out, would it?" Jeff pleaded.

"Jeff, you say it's a case of severe brain damage? I've had a lot of experience with brain-damaged patients, but . . . "

Jeff interruped. "Dr. Walt, I have lots of money in the bank. I'll pay you plenty if you'll just try. Don't you see? If Mark were well again, that would solve everything."

Dr. Walt studied Jeff carefully. "You're very anxious to help the Herrons, aren't you?"

Terry spoke up softly. "He's got a monkey on his back." Quickly he told about Jeff's parents' accident.

"That's why he wants to help the Herrons get back to Colombia, so they'll take his parents' place, telling the people about Jesus."

"Thanks for filling me in," the doctor said. Then he turned to Jeff. "Does anyone else believe it's your fault?"

"Oh, no. Terry tells me I'm crazy to blame myself. And Mr. Herron says so too."

"But you don't believe them, do you?" said the doctor.

"I still have nightmares," Jeff answered sadly.

"Jeff, listen carefully. Who has the power of life and death? Who?" the doctor asked.

"Why, God, I guess," Jeff answered slowly.

The doctor nodded. "God. That's right. But you say it's your fault that your parents are dead?" Then the doctor looked Jeff in the eyes. "Jeff, are you trying to play God?"

He paused, giving Jeff time to think. Then he went on. "Playing God is serious business. No way can you or I or anyone else change God's timing for life or death. No one! Do you understand that, Jeff?"

Jeff frowned. "Me, trying to play God? That's wrong."

"Yes," the doctor agreed. "Now, why don't you ask God to forgive you? Would you like to ask Him to change your mind, to 'heal' your thinking?"

Jeff nodded. They all bowed their heads as Jeff prayed, "Dear Lord, please forgive me for saying it was my fault that my parents died. And please forgive me for trying to play God. May I never do it again. And please heal my thinking so I won't blame myself for my parents' death anymore. In Jesus' name I ask this, Amen."

"Amen," the Doctor repeated. "And now, Jeff, when we ask God to forgive us, what does He do?"

"Why, He forgives us, of course!" answered Jeff.

"Right! He forgives us. No more should you have any guilt feelings. No more should you have any nightmares. *Already* He has forgiven you. Isn't that great?"

Suddenly the doctor glanced at his watch. "Got to hurry. Oh, by the way, I'd like to see Mr. Herron before the meeting. Let's go."

A few minutes later they all met him in Mr. Perry's office. First, Mr. Herron introduced the boys to Mr. Perry. Then Jeff said to Mr. Herron, "This is Dr. Walt Willoughby. He was painting with us. He's a psychiatrist and may be able to help Mark."

Dr. Walt laughed. "Slow down, Son. You're way ahead of yourself."

When everyone had said hello, Mr. Perry said, "Well, Jim, since our business is almost completed, why don't you and Dr. Walt go over to the table in the corner and talk. I'll visit with the boys here till you get done."

When the two men had left, Mr. Perry drew up chairs for Jeff and Terry.

"Jim Herron's been telling me what a great job you've been doing with Mark," Mr. Perry said. "You're great therapy for him. How do you like helping?"

"At first I didn't like it at all," Jeff admitted. "I wanted a brother I could do things with."

"But you changed your mind and decided to help?" questioned Mr. Perry.

"Yes! I want the Herrons to get back to Colombia.

If Mark can get help here, maybe the Herrons can go."

"Or," Terry added, "if the right doctor was down at the base, Mark could go back with his parents."

"Hmmm!" The man leaned far back in his chair, rubbed his chin, and frowned. "Jim's a great help to the other translators down there," he said. "They desperately need him to finish that New Testament."

"Well, they *could* leave Mark here somewhere," Jeff said slowly, "but they don't have the money."

The man moved forward and leaned on the desk. "Putting him in a home? Yes, Jim told me he would if it were God's will. But the boy has shown so much improvement. What might happen if he were taken away from the love and care of his mom, dad, and brother?"

"His brother?" Jeff frowned. "He doesn't have one."

Terry turned and grinned. "Hey, man. Aren't *you* just like his brother now?"

Jeff felt as if he were in a dense fog. That was a new idea, that he, Jeff, was all that important in Mark's recovery. He'd have to think that one over.

But he had no time to think just then. Mr. Herron and Dr. Walt had finished talking. As they walked over to the desk, the doctor was saying, "I'll phone in a few days before I come."

"You're going to treat Mark?" Jeff asked anxiously.

Dr. Walt put his hand on Jeff's shoulder. "I just want to meet him, Jeff. I don't have any miracles up my sleeve!"

"Well, you never *know!*" Jeff persisted, as everyone else smiled.

Chapter 10

Trapped!

After the group prayer meeting, Mr. Perry took them all to lunch. Then Mr. Herron and the boys drove home.

By that time Jeff and Terry were ready to do one thing: check up on possible bank robbers. Soon they had their rock sacks loaded and took off without telling anyone where they were going.

But when they got to the end of the dirt road, Terry started to laugh. "You know we're crazy!"

Jeff tossed his head. The heavy shock of hair that usually fell over his eye, flipped back. "How come?" he asked a little impatiently.

"We see three guys taking a hike," said Terry. "We hear that three guys robbed a bank. And we want the reward money so badly we think the hikers *have* to be the bank robbers. I tell you, we're crazy!"

"But they looked so guilty!" Jeff insisted. "They acted so mad that we'd seen them. And what about their shoes? One guy with old, torn sneakers. The tall one with shiny black shoes on—you know, the kind you use for dress up. And you said yourself they didn't know anything about hiking."

Now it was Terry's turn to frown. "Hiking in rough country in sneakers is about as dumb as playing football in bedroom slippers."

Terry stood up, grabbing his sack of stuff. "OK, let's go. I don't know, though."

To Jeff it seemed hotter than it had the day before; the path seemed dustier; the trail seemed steeper. And when the trail seemed steeper. And when the trail climbed the canyon wall, each boulder seemed intent on nudging the boys closer to the edge.

The birds were silent, the air quiet. It was as if all nature were holding its breath.

Terry stopped and looked around. Jeff wondered if Terry also felt as if 1,000 eyes were watching them.

He glanced down at the creek bed far below. From where they were, high on the cliffside, they couldn't even see it.

On they went. "We're getting closer," Terry whispered. "Don't kick over any rocks. If the men are here, they'll know we're coming."

Jeff shifted the pack on his back. Then he took the lead. When they finally came to the last bend, Jeff signaled to stop. Then he inched up, his face close to the edge of the cliff. When he peeked around, the small flat area below the mine looked deserted.

"Anyone there?" Terry whispered.

"No one. Let's go!" Jeff answered.

Everything seemed the same. High above them was the mine entrance, hidden by the pile of rock and dirt in front of it.

"A good place to hide," Jeff said, nodding toward a thick clump of bushes off to their right.

Terry squinted in that direction. "Yeah. Hey, what are we going to do, stand here gawking all day?"

Silent as Indian braves stalking buffalo, the boys started up: slowly, carefully, so no one would hear them—that is, if anyone were around to hear.

First they'd head one way, then the other, as the trail snaked back and forth up the face of the slope. And even though the sun's rays must have been at least 120°, Jeff felt a cold shiver run down his back. Bank robbing was dangerous enough. But recovering the bankrobbers' loot for the reward . . . Well, if they got caught . . .

Finally the boys crawled the last few feet. Again they were on the tiny flat, the entrance to Dead Man's Mine. Again Jeff noticed the post, its sign long since ripped off. He noticed the boulder too. Someday it would be fun to send it crashing down the cliff. But certainly not now.

For a few minutes the two just lay puffing. "Think anyone's inside?" asked Terry.

For an answer, Jeff crawled closer. Slowly he stuck his head around the wall of rock. "Can't hear a thing."

"Come on, then. Let's go inside," Terry said.

Pulling out their flashlights filled with new batteries, the boys started in. They hardly felt the air cool down as they headed deep into the dark tunnel.

"Didn't see a thing," Jeff moaned when they got to the end. "What do you think they did with the bags?"

"Could they have buried them in here somewhere?" asked Terry.

"Most of the floor's solid rock. Hey, what about that stuff we dug out yesterday?" asked Jeff.

Instantly they headed for the third tunnel on the left. The pile of rubble they had made seemed undisturbed. Just the same, Jeff started digging into it with his pick.

"Something soft! A flight bag!" Jeff shouted.

Terry was digging away too. "And here's another!"

For another few minutes they dug furiously. Soon they were down to solid rock.

"No third bag," Terry murmured. But Jeff was opening his up.

"Hey, look. All $10 bills!" shouted Jeff.

"I got all $20s," Terry said excitedly. "And some $50s too."

Jeff couldn't stop shaking. "I've never seen this much money in my whole life."

"Oh, I don't know," Terry quipped. "My pop gives me this much for my allowance every week."

"*Now* who's talking crazy?" Jeff said, laughing. But it was a hollow laugh. "Hey, let's get out of here, and quick."

First they strapped on their rock sacks once more. Then, ducking to keep from hitting their heads, they dashed for the entrance and plunged out into the brilliant sunlight.

"Oh, my eyes," Jeff groaned. Then suddenly he screamed, as he felt himself slipping over the edge of the cliff.

"Help!" he yelled in terror, as he came to a stop on his side against a boulder.

"Don't move! I'm coming," called Terry.

Jeff hung on for dear life as he waited for help.

Suddenly a voice called, "Who's up there?"

Just then Terry dropped his belt over the ledge. "Grab it," he yelled to Jeff. Terry moved till his upper half was mostly over the edge.

"Got it," Jeff gasped.

"Pull yourself up," Terry yelled, "but do it slowly and turn over on your stomach."

From below them the voice came again. "OK you guys, throw down the flight bags, or I'm coming up after you."

"Watch out!" came a frightened cry from somewhere. "He's got a gun!"

"Shut up, kid," said the man to the other voice. Then he shouted again, "Come on. Throw those bags down!"

"Who was that other voice?" Jeff asked.

"Come on," urged Terry. "Pull yourself up! I can't hang on much longer."

Jeff gripped the buckle and then, wriggling like a snake on its belly, inched his way up.

"Don't jerk. You're pulling me over," warned Terry.

By the time the man got to the bottom of the mine trail, Jeff had eased his legs up over the edge. Both boys lay there exhausted.

"I'm coming up," the man shouted.

Jeff shivered as Terry moved to the edge.

"Poing!" a bullet bounced off the rocks. Terry ducked back. "Hey, that guy's not kidding."

Although Jeff knew he shouldn't, he peeked over too. "Hey, he's got the third flight bag. No wonder we didn't find it."

For a moment they lay there, hugging the ground. "What'll we do?" Jeff wanted to know.

Terry whispered, "I'm praying."

"Me too," said Jeff.

And as they prayed, they heard the bank robber yelling and puffing, scrambling up towards them.

"Right now, we need a miracle!" said Jeff.

"But don't expect a miracle if you've got a means," Terry reminded Jeff, remembering what Mr. Herron had told them.

"A means. But what?" asked Jeff.

From where they lay the boys studied the ground in every direction. "Too bad this bag isn't heavier," Jeff murmured. "We could throw it down on him. Might slow him up a bit."

"Hey, what about that rock?" asked Terry.

"You mean, roll that boulder down on him?" questioned Jeff. "That could *kill* him."

Terry frowned. "He's shooting at *us*, isn't he? We could get killed!"

Jeff wiggled uneasily. Terry was right, though. The man surely meant them harm. They crawled over to the boulder and tried to shove it, but it was too heavy. "Why don't we push it with our feet?" suggested Terry.

The boys flipped over on their backs, and shoved. Little by little the boulder inched closer to the edge. They both gave one last push, then stood up to watch. The boulder crashed down, down, down.

"Watch out!" Jeff shouted.

The man looked up and cursed. The rock didn't really roll all that close, but he jumped anyway. Landing too close to the edge of the trail, his arms flew up. The flight bag and gun went flying into the air. Almost before they knew it, the man's heavy body thudded onto the switchback, 10 to 15 feet below.

"Oh, my leg!" the man yelled. "It's broken!"

Jeff and Terry looked at each other. They gripped hands. "Thanks, Lord! Thanks for a miracle!"

"Hey, you guys," came the other voice from the bushes. "Come, cut me loose."

The boys frowned. They had heard the voice before. But where?

Quickly they scrambled down. For the moment, they darted past the injured man on the trail.

"Over here, guys," the voice came again.

"It's Ritter!" Terry shouted. Hands tied behind his back, and feet tied to a bush, Ritter wasn't going anywhere.

While they untied him, he explained. "I came up early this morning to dig gold where you found some yesterday. But that guy caught me."

Jeff felt a little angry. Ritter was always trying to cut in on their business. Still, he *had* warned them that the man had a gun, and right now there were other things to think about.

Quickly the boys went to the injured man. Although he no longer had a gun, only Terry went close.

"Sorry, about the boulder," he said quietly. "But you were shooting at us."

"Get help. Hurry. I'm bleeding!" the man whimpered.

"I know about bleeding," Terry said. "I'm a scout. Let me look."

Jeff and Ritter watched from the switchback below. If the man tried any tricks, at least they wouldn't be caught and could run for help.

Suddenly the man grabbed Terry's arm. "Tell your friends to get my flight bag."

Jeff and Ritter watched, fearfully. The man might have a broken leg, but he still could hurt Terry if he tried. But why did he want the bag? Was there another gun inside?

Jeff went over to where the bag had fallen. Quickly he zipped it open. "It's a CB unit," he called to Terry.

Terry spoke to the man quietly, "You're bleeding, mister. Do you want help, or do you want to stay here?"

"Turn on Channel 9. Emergency. Tell 'em to come quick," said the man.

"Jeff," Terry's voice quivered just a bit, "don't call till he turns me loose."

The man turned into a volcano, spewing out threats and curses. Jeff prayed. Suddenly Terry wrenched free.

From a safe distance away, he said, "We'll call for help now. Your bleeding is just from a small cut. You're not bleeding to death. You'll be OK."

Jeff switched the CB on, hoping it had not been damaged by the fall. Turning to Channel 9, he called: "Emergency! Emergency! Send help. Man down on trail with broken leg at Dead Man's Mine. Repeat. Man with broken leg. Dead Man's Mine. We need help. Does anyone read me? Answer, please."

He switched to listen. They waited a bit. Soon the message came.

"Portable unit at Dead Man's Mine. Portable unit at the mine. This is REACT. We read you loud and clear. Will phone the sheriff immediately. Get back to you in a minute."

For a moment the fellows relaxed. "Think we'll get a reward?" Jeff wondered.

But even before Terry could answer, they heard footsteps coming round the bend in the trail below. In a moment, the boys saw the other two men who'd been on the trail the day before.

"Reward?" Terry gasped as he started running. "Hey, man. We'll be lucky to get out of here alive."

All three of the boys struggled back up the trail toward the mine like mountain goats running from a hunter.

"Why go up there?" Jeff gasped. "It's a dead-end."

For a moment Terry stopped. "Oh, no!"

They looked back. The tall man with the mustache was bent over the man with the broken leg. The third man, the smaller one, was coming after the boys.

"Come on," Terry cried. "Dead-end or no dead-end, here we come."

Up they scrambled. Finally, they were at the entrance to Dead Man's Mine.

Terry picked up the flight bag he'd left there and looked around. The third man was still climbing. He was slow, but he'd get them sooner or later.

Quickly Jeff scanned the slope above. No trail of any sort. But up another 100 feet, and to the side, there seemed to be a tiny flat. Maybe they could get there.

"Here. Let me carry the bag," Jeff yelled, as they all took off up the barren slope.

The boys clawed at the hillside for footholds as they tried to escape. In a few more seconds, the robber was standing safely on the flat they had just left.

"OK, kid. Throw down the bag," he shouted, waving a gun.

Jeff glanced back. The man was only yards away. Then he looked ahead at Terry and Ritter. They were grabbing at anything they could and struggling to hang on.

Suddenly Jeff heard a shot. And almost at the same instant, he screamed in terror. The rock beneath him had been blasted away. He was slipping down, down, down. The flight bag went flying.

"Spread eagle, Jeff. Spread eagle!" Terry yelled. Jeff obeyed, and his sliding stopped. His toe felt around for something solid. The man started down the trail again.

For a bit the boys lay still, as if glued to the cliffside. Then they started inching up again. The slope was steep. The going was slow. Any misstep could send them tumbling down. But at least the men couldn't get to them there. However, it was getting darker all the time.

Finally Jeff and Terry reached the safety of the ledge. Both of them sprawled flat, gasping for breath.

"Hey, where's Ritter?" Terry asked.

"He was with us a minute ago," answered Jeff.

Right away they crawled to the edge. Straining their eyes in the dark, they finally spotted a blob about 10 feet below.

"Hey, Ritter. You all right?" asked Terry.

"Help!" came the frightened whisper. "If I move, I'm gone."

Terry rolled over, digging his light out of his sack. He flashed it down and they could see Ritter hanging on, both hands clamped around a scrawny little bush. One foot was pushing against a small rock. The other was hanging out over empty space.

"Dear God, don't let him fall!" Terry prayed aloud.

"But what can we do? There's no foothold at all between him and us. And it's so steep," said Jeff.

Terry's voice sounded calm. "Ritter, we'll save you. Just hang on."

"But how?" Jeff whispered.

"I don't know yet. Keep praying."

"Dear Lord," Jeff began aloud. "Please help us rescue Ritter. Please don't let him fall. And keep us from getting hurt too."

"Amen!" said Terry. "Now, get out your pick. If we dig the pick in the cliff, and hang on, we won't slide."

"But how can we pull ourselves up?" asked Jeff.

"That'll be plenty hard. But here's what we'll do."

After explaining it carefully, Terry called down. "Ritter, we're coming. Hang on!"

"Hurry," came the weak answer from below. "I can't hang on much longer."

Terry reached far over the edge and dug his pick in deep. Slowly he eased himself down. In a minute he was crouched over the pick.

"Come on," he told Jeff. "Climb down over me. Dig your pick in at my feet. But stay as flat on the ground as you can."

Jeff struggled down. Finally he dug his pick in just under Terry's feet. Then he let his body down as far as he could, still hanging on to the pick.

Terry called out, "Ritter, grab Jeff's legs. Keep as flat as you can."

"I can't let go. I'll fall," Ritter answered in a scared voice.

"You've got to do what I say. Now, hurry!" Terry ordered.

Jeff hugged the part of the pick that was out of the ground. Suddenly a hand grabbed his ankle. Jeff thought he would loose his grip. "Lord, help!" he gasped.

Suddenly Ritter's other hand clamped onto Jeff's other leg. Jeff thought he would be wrenched apart. He squeezed his eyes shut and hugged the pick.

"Keep your body on the ground," Terry coached from above. "Spread eagle."

Slowly Jeff felt Ritter pulling himself up. Now he was grabbing at his belt. Jeff felt as though his stomach were being cut in half. Then a hand clawed at his shoulder. After a bit, a huge shoe jammed down in his face. Jeff nearly let go because of the pain. But just when he thought he couldn't take anymore, the foot moved.

Jeff just lay there, weak. Ritter had made it. But after all that, could he?

When Ritter reached the top, he lay flat and reached his belt down to Terry. Hanging on to that with one hand, Terry was able to reach down and give Jeff a hand.

When Jeff and Terry were finally safe, Ritter gasped, "You guys saved my life. Thanks!"

Everyone was panting hard. Finally Jeff said, "Thank God! He's the One who helped us make it."

"I heard you guys praying," Ritter said slowly. "Do you *really* believe in that stuff?"

"If God hadn't given us the courage," Terry panted, "we would have been too scared to try. Look down that slope."

"No thanks." Ritter shivered.

For a while the three just lay still, gasping for air. As the sun sank behind the hills, the wind began to chill their bodies. The boys huddled together to keep warm. There was barely room for the three of them on the ledge.

Suddenly, they heard the drone of a rescue helicopter. As it came over the hills, it moved slowly, trying to find the trail with its powerful spotlight.

"We've got to signal them," said Jeff, reaching for his light.

Quickly the copter moved up and hovered over them. The two officers inside pointed down to where the injured man was lying. It circled carefully, then settled on a clear spot below.

The boys watched as two lights moved from the copter to the man. Then a light turned in their direction. One of the rescue squad officers spoke through a bullhorn. "You boys OK?"

"We're OK," Jeff shouted, "but we can't get down."

"Stay where you are. After we take care of this man, we'll come for you," ordered the officer from the rescue squad.

The boys watched as the officers strapped the man in a stretcher and secured it to the chopper. Slowly the pilot eased off and was gone.

The officer started toward the boys. He didn't have the bullhorn now, only his strong light and some rope and a pick.

Before he took a step, he drove the pick deep into the ground. He could hold onto the end while he climbed higher.

Even he was puffing hard by the time he reached the ledge where the boys were waiting.

"What in the world are you doing up here?" he asked when he reached them. "Don't you realize how dangerous this is?"

"Those bank robbers were chasing us," Jeff explained. "We found their money in the mine."

"They had me all tied up," Ritter added.

"What are you talking about?" the officer asked. "The man down there said you were stuck up here on the ledge. You yelled for help, and he tried to save you, but he slipped."

"No way!" Terry argued. "Those guys are the bank robbers. We found their two flight bags full of money in the mine."

"But there's only one man down there and he has a broken leg. And all he had with him was a CB unit."

"But, Officer," Jeff said.

"Save your breath, kid. We'll find out the truth when we all get out of here." The officer sounded quite disbelieving.

No one said anything for a few minutes. Then the officer spoke. "When the chopper gets back, I'll take you down. They can hold a light on us from below. Easier that way. By the way, you say you were in the mine?"

"Yeah. That's where we found the money," said Terry.

"Didn't you read the sign?" the officer asked gruffly.

"It's not there anymore," said Jeff. "Just the post."

"Well, the sign said, 'Danger. No Trespassing! Keep out!' You could have been killed in there. You're old enough to know that without a sign. Don't you have any sense?

"You can also get into plenty of trouble for calling out the rescue squad to get you. Costs the county lots of money for one of these operations. The officials don't like spending it for rescuing people who do dumb things they know they shouldn't be doing in the first place."

The boys were silent as they waited. Jeff felt lower than a caterpillar's hind foot. He and Terry had started out to catch the bank robbers, or at least to find the money they stole. But now, they were being treated like lawbreakers themselves.

When the chopper returned, the officer tied a rope around each of the boys' waists, then his own. First he drove a spike deep into the ground, anchoring his rope to it. Then he let himself down. The boys followed. A few feet at a time, the officer guided and protected them all the way.

It took two chopper trips to get them all back to the sheriff's station. The ride through the dark mountains, then over the brilliant lights of town would have been exciting. But the boys felt so depressed, they didn't enjoy it at all.

At the station they had to tell their story all over again while one of the officers called Mr. Herron. Jeff felt himself getting angry inside when the officers still didn't believe them. Then he remembered something. "I even got their license number," he told them, digging into his wallet. "DRP-479. That was the car at the bottom of the hill when we came back from the mine the first time."

The desk sergeant frowned as he took the slip. "We'll check this number out, then we'll see you boys again. In the meantime, don't get into any more trouble."

By then, Mr. Herron had arrived to take them home.

Chapter 11

Making Miracles Happen

A few days later Jeff and Terry were again sitting at the picnic table in the cool shade of the giant maple. Mark would be done with his nap in a few minutes and they were there to take care of him. Uncle Marv and Aunt Flo were indoors with Aunt Matty.

Jeff was glad the Dead Man's Mine episode was over—or almost over. The sheriff still hadn't called.

"You know," he said, "at the beginning of the summer I wanted a brother to have fun with."

"Instead, you got Mark," Terry said. "Still sorry he came?"

"I was at first, real sorry," Jeff answered slowly. "But I guess helping someone can be just as much fun—not in the same way, of course."

Terry nodded. "Think you'll miss him?"

"Miss him?" echoed Jeff. "Why, the Herrons have been like a whole new family to me. Maybe *I* needed *them* even more than Mark needed me."

For a while the boys were silent. Jeff felt as if a part of him would soon be cut off. He'd known that feeling before, when his parents died. That feeling of being all alone, empty, deserted.

"Hey, Jeff. What about that monkey on your back?"

"It's been gone since that day I asked God to forgive me for trying to take over His job."

"That's great!" answered Terry.

Just then a car headed down the long drive. It was their new friend, Dr. Walt.

Soon everyone was gathered around the picnic table. Aunt Matty came slowly from the house to join them. From behind the bushes, Ritter appeared too. "Mind if I join you?" he asked.

After visiting for a few moments, Mrs. Herron took Mark inside the apartment where Dr. Walt examined him.

"He's got a good healthy body," the doctor said as they came out.

"Now, I'm not a neurologist, but I used to work with brain-damaged people a lot. If the Herrons are willing to let me try to help Mark, my wife and I have been given permission to do our short-term work in Colombia with the Herrons."

Suddenly everyone was smiling and crying at the same time. The Herrons, of course, were delighted to hear this news and Jeff and Terry were just as happy.

Just then a black and white car came up the drive.

An officer got out. "Jeff Palmer? Terry Miller? Ritter Colombo? You're wanted down at headquarters." The three boys climbed into the car.

"I'll bring them back in a couple of hours," the sheriff told the others as he started away.

When the boys returned to Aunt Matty's farm, they

were smiling. "Thanks a lot, Officer," Jeff yelled as they stepped out of the patrol car.

"No more exploring mines, you guys," the officer said, but with a grin.

"OK. That's a promise," the boys answered.

The Herron family, followed by Aunt Matty, Aunt Flo, and Uncle Marv, hurried out to meet them.

"They checked up on that license number I gave them," Jeff yelled, running toward the group. "They caught one of the guys. The other one got away with the money, though, so it looks like we won't get any reward. Still, they might find the third guy . . . "

"I'm glad that's over," Aunt Matty sighed. "I don't like you boys in trouble with the police."

Terry grinned. "Neither do we!"

Jeff looked around. "Everything is working out, isn't it," he said slowly. But he felt unhappy for he knew he was going to miss the Herrons.

Just then Mr. Herron laid his hand on Jeff's shoulder. "There's still one problem, Son." Jeff looked up. The man's face was troubled.

"Oh, no," thought Jeff. "First good news, then bad." Jeff's insides were churning again.

"Dr. Walt doesn't think he can help Mark much unless he has the help of the right therapist," Mr. Herron said.

"Therapist? What's that?" asked Jeff.

"That's sort of a doctor's helper, isn't it?" Terry asked.

"Oh, no!" Jeff groaned inside. Always something seemed to go wrong—always another problem to solve.

"Maybe we could have another Gopher Hole Treasure Hunt," he suggested, not really knowing what to say. "Maybe a therapist would read another story and volunteer."

"Oh, not just ANY therapist," said Mr. Herron, smiling in a secret sort of way. "Dr. Walt knows just the one he wants. But he doesn't know if this person would be willing yet."

"But can't you talk him into going?" Jeff wondered. "Who is this guy, anyway?"

"*You*, Jeff! Dr. Walt wants you!"

Jeff couldn't believe what he had just heard. "Me? But I'm not a trained therapist. And I'm only a kid."

"But that's just the reason you'd be the right helper," said Dr. Walt. "Mark needs someone your age to be with—a brother. You'd be a great help to him and me. Your Aunt Matty and Uncle Marv say you may go. WA Headquarters says it can be arranged. It's up to you, Jeff!"

Jeff felt his heart pounding all the way from his head to his toes.

Terry laughed. And even Ritter was smiling. "All you've got to do is say 'Yes,' old buddy!" Terry said.

Jeff felt his eyes fill with tears—happy tears. Then he whispered, " 'In everything you do, put God first, and He will direct you and crown your efforts with success.' "

Terry grinned. "I like that verse. That's just what God did. He crowned our efforts with success. He got a home for Mark—the best in the world, his own."

"Yes," Jeff said happily, "and now He's giving me a home too—in Colombia—where I belong."